CAPE HOPE CAPERS

CAPE HOPE MYSTERIES

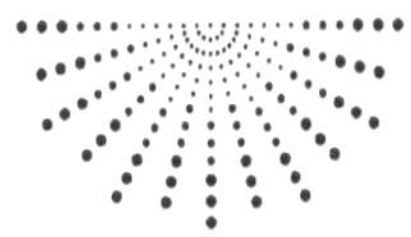

WINNIE REED

CAPE HOPE CAPERS

CAPE HOPE MYSTERIES BOOK FOUR

An antique book. A mysterious old photo. Emma's curiosity and perseverance and an old mystery about Cape Hope's royalty.

Join Emma on her next adventure with the adorable Lola, Detective McHottie, and a certain photographer who's decided to make an appearance.

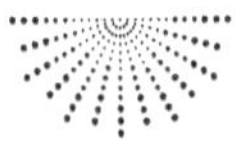

"How many old horror books can a bookstore hold?" I wondered aloud, plopping another paperback on top of the ever-growing stack. "It's like there was a purge and everybody decided to get rid of them at once."

My sister snickered. "This didn't just happen. These books have been traded in for store credit for, like, ever. Since I opened the store and decided it would be a fabulous idea to offer credit for used books."

She looked around at the piles and piles of books all around us with a heavy sigh. "And voila. Here we are. Combing through them to see what I can give away."

"You're making space for new inventory," I pointed out with a smile. "Isn't that great?"

"Who are you and what have you done with my sister?" she laughed. "Since when are you a Pollyanna?"

"I would hardly call myself a Pollyanna," I retorted. "And I don't have to spend my Monday night doing this with you, either." I glanced out the window, noting the growing darkness. It was almost nine o'clock, but there was still light enough to see by out there.

Weird. I could never live someplace like Sweden or Alaska, where the sun was up late at night.

"What else would you have done?" Darcy asked, all smug-like and older-sisterly.

"Ew!" I stuck out my tongue. "Don't act all superior just because you have a boyfriend now."

"I've told you, Karl's not my boyfriend."

"Oh! He has a name now? I'm allowed to know his name? I'm honored."

"Anyway, he's not my boyfriend. Not yet." She could try all she wanted, but my sister couldn't hide from me. She tried to turn her face away before I could see her frown, but it was no use.

"What's his issue? What, he's too stupid to see what a catch you are? How stupid it would be to let you get away? Do I need to have a talk with him?"

She blanched. "No, for God's sake, anything but that."

"Thanks for the vote of confidence."

"I don't mean that, idiot." She picked up a handful of paperbacks and started sorting them out. "I mean, I don't want him to feel pressured."

"Oh, we wouldn't want that. We wouldn't want him to feel like there's any need to tell you what's on his mind, whether he wants the two of you to be an actual item or not. Wouldn't want him to take your feelings into consideration."

"Are we still talking about me?" she asked. "Or somebody I know?"

"I'm talking about you, obviously." This time, I was the one looking away, neatly piling a dozen books so they wouldn't fall over. Like my life depended on them staying upright.

"Because you sound a little too passionate. Like you have a personal problem along these lines."

"Well, I don't," I murmured.

"So you're not even a little annoyed that Deke hasn't confirmed when he's coming to town—or even if he definitely is, since he hasn't committed?"

"He's coming this week. I know he is." And I almost dreaded it, seeing as how Joe Sullivan was already staying in town.

I didn't have any commitment to either of these men.

Heck, I could barely spend ten minutes with Joe without wanting to do something that would only result in my arrest. And Deke? He floated to and fro on the breeze, going from place to place on assignment for Haute Cuisine and randomly flying to France at the drop of a hat.

They were both enough to make me want to give up on men forever.

Why did it bother me so much, the thought of them being in town together? Like spending time with one meant being unfaithful to the other? I owed nothing to either of them, except friendship and gratitude since they'd both helped me through difficult times and had probably saved my bacon more than once.

Darcy only smirked as she stacked another pile of used books. "Without you knowing if he wants the two of you to be a thing?"

"A thing?" I snorted. "I don't wanna be a thing."

"Don't get all cute with me, Emma. You know what I mean. You want to know what he's thinking. Whether he wants something for you guys, instead of him drifting in and out of your life."

"He made it sound like he does," I reminded her. "When I talked to him last week."

"Before you found that body floating in the pool, at the casino."

"Exactly. Thanks for bringing that delightful memory back."

"Anyway, don't get all annoyed on my account when it's your account you're more upset over. You're in limbo and limbo has never been your favorite place."

"Is it anybody's favorite place?" I asked the ceiling. The ceiling didn't have an answer for me, but I preferred its silence to my sister's know-it-all smartypants attitude.

I pulled another bunch of books my way rather than continuing with this pointless discussion. "Whew. Musty."

"Some of these books are so old," she agreed. "I know there's been one or two times when somebody's died and whoever was in charge of packing their things brought the books here. I didn't want to tell them not to bother. I hate to see books getting thrown away."

"What do you plan on doing with these?" I asked.

"Not throwing them out, if that's what you're trying to ask. There are all kinds of places to donate books. Schools, prisons, halfway houses, that sort of thing."

"Well, I hope they like horror, whoever they are." I picked up an old, hardback book whose title I couldn't make out. The dust jacket was nowhere to be found, and whoever the book had belonged to had rubbed the letters pressed into the cover until they were illegible.

Something about that intrigued me. This was a beloved book. Somebody had sat down with it so many times, running their hands over the cover. I'd had a lot of books like that over the years. The ones I could read over and over.

"You think I could have this one?" I asked, still examining the cover.

"Sure. Which one is it?"

"I don't know." I looked up at her, fully aware of how strange I sounded. "It's not even about that. It's about somebody loving this book. They loved it. It meant a lot to them."

"How do you know that?" She wasn't kidding anymore, though. Her voice went soft. If anybody could understand what it meant to love a book, it would be my sister. The bookstore owner.

"They rubbed the letters off the cover. See? And the pages are worn, too." I flipped them to show her. And I noticed a stiffness toward the end. Like something was tucked in there.

"Ooh, a picture!" I worked it out from between the pages.

"Let me see!"

"Wait your turn," I muttered, pulling my arm away. Maybe not my most mature moment, but what did I care? I was studying an old picture.

It was black-and-white, on thicker paper than I was used to seeing pictures printed on. A girl stood in the foreground, off to the right, wearing a pretty, floaty sort of dress. One hand rested on her belly.

Her very pregnant belly.

She wasn't looking down at it, though, not like some women did in their pregnancy photos. Instead, she looked off into the distance, toward the left of the frame.

"She's so pretty," Darcy mused from over my shoulder. "But she looks…"

"Sad," I whispered. "She looks so sad."

"Don't go jumping to conclusions."

"What were you gonna say?" I asked, elbowing her. "She looks what?"

"Like she's about to pop. Very pregnant."

And sad. She looked very sad. It didn't matter what Darcy said. There was a wistful look in the girl's eyes. "I wonder when it was taken. I wonder if maybe the baby's father died or something. Like in the war."

"There goes your imagination."

"I'm a writer."

"You write about food," Darcy pointed out.

"Okay, fine, maybe she was thinking about a piece of pie she just ate. Maybe she already missed it and wished there was more. Is that better?"

She burst out laughing. "Yeah, terrific. Well, she's standing in front of the Montbatten house, so she was prob-ably well-off."

"She could've been a servant there, right? And there's no ring on her left hand."

"Hmm. True."

"I wonder who she was. I wonder if she was ever happy

after she had her baby." I was already thinking about her, making up stories in my head. Darcy was right—my imagination was already getting ahead of me.

"She probably was." Darcy shrugged. "I mean, if everything went well."

"Now I just have to know." I flipped the photo over. The back was blank. There was nothing else stuck in the pages of the book, which according to the title page was *The Scarlett Letter.*

I pointed to it. "Now, tell me that doesn't mean anything. Here's a picture of what looks like an unmarried woman carrying a baby, and it was tucked into this particular book. Come on. Tell me that doesn't intrigue you."

"I'm pretty sure you need a hobby," Darcy snickered. "Come on. I'd like to get through with this sometime tonight." I made it a point to put the book aside so it didn't get lost before getting back to work.

"So," my beloved sister grinned as we packed the books in boxes, "when are you getting together with Joe?"

"Who says I'm getting together with him?" I tried to move a box, but she stopped me.

"You have to take it easy on that wrist, remember?" The wrist I'd sprained falling into an empty pool. Falling wasn't the right word, exactly. I'd launched myself at the woman threatening to shoot her literary agent and me, and we landed in the empty pool together. Leave it to my sister to keep an eye on me.

She continued after placing that full box on top of another. "I do, because I know you. And Mom said he was very familiar and friendly when he came into tell you he was around for the week."

"I'm sure Mom worked in a bunch of details that didn't really happen, too. Did he bring me flowers? Did he ride up to the café on a literal white stallion? Was his shirt half-unbuttoned to show off his rippling chest?" I batted my eyelashes and pretended to swoon.

"Wow, it's like you were there when she told me," she laughed.

I was shaking my head when my phone buzzed. And boy, did I dislike the way my heart jumped into my throat at the thought of it being Joe. Only it wasn't—though the man who'd sent the text was the first important man in my life.

"Hey—it's Dad," I announced.

"Oh?" Darcy suddenly became very interested in a piece of lint on her t-shirt.

"Wants us to come for dinner tomorrow night."

"Good for him." That had to be an incredibly tough piece of lint. Invisible, too, since I couldn't see it. But she kept picking at it, absorbed.

"Darce."

"Em." Her eyes met mine under lowered brows. "Why are you so insistent on giving me grief over this? Why can't you just let it go?"

"Why can't I just let it go that you won't speak to our father because he, God forbid, found a girlfriend after divorcing Mom? Why does that bother me? Because you're my family, for starters."

She heaved a put-upon sigh, stacking more books.

"We're still your family, even when I don't feel like talking to him. Especially not when he's with his little girlfriend."

His little girlfriend. My head was starting to hurt. "Her name is Holly, and you know it. She's a pretty substantial person. A businesswoman—you know how that goes. And she loves him. Plus, she makes a mean red sauce."

"Fabulous." She held up her hands, palms out. "I don't wanna talk about this. You know it. I don't see why it's so hard for you to understand that."

"I only want us to get along, that's all."

"You can't make people get along. You can't save everybody. This is one fight you won't be able to win. Sorry about that."

She didn't sound very sorry. I decided to let it go, since banging my head against a brick wall wasn't exactly something I enjoyed as a pastime.

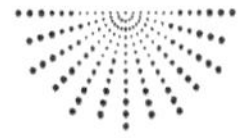

"How's your wrist, hon?" Dad examined my bandaged wrist with a deep frown. "You're lucky you didn't break it."

"I know, I know." I accepted his hug, leaning against him. No matter how independent I was, no matter how old I got, there was nothing quite like a hug from my dad. "But it could've been a lot worse than that, too. A broken wrist is nothing compared to a hole in the head."

"Oh, Emma!" Holly gasped, turning away from the oven with a piping-hot lasagna. "Don't even talk like that!"

My father then said the very last thing I would've expected. "Let's change the subject."

My eyebrows almost shot right up off my head. "I'm sorry. Where's my dad? What have you done with him?"

He shot me a warning look. "For once, I wanna lay off you, and you're wondering why I don't come down harder. Explain that one to me."

"Okay, fine. Far be it from me to look a gift horse in the

mouth." I got back to work smearing garlic butter on two halves of a loaf of bread, which Holly then placed in the oven to bake. My mouth watered at the aroma.

"I saw somebody familiar in town earlier today," Dad reported in a far-too-casual tone.

"Oh? Who's that?"

"The detective from Paradise City. Joe What's-His-Name."

"Oh? That's nice. He told me he'd be in town this week when he stopped by the café yesterday morning. He needs rest after a panic attack he had last week."

"Oh, poor guy." Holly shook her head, glancing at Dad. "Work-related?" She was probably thinking about him, wondering if he was liable to have the same trouble. Cape Hope was a far cry from Paradise City.

"Yeah, it was during the investigation into the death at the resort. Hundreds and hundreds of conference attendees, anybody could've been responsible. He didn't look good before the attack. And he ended up in the ER, thinking his heart was going out on him."

"Poor guy," Holly mused again. "You seem pretty aware of what went on."

We exchanged a knowing look which my father seemed to miss. I liked Holly a lot. Unlike Darcy, I saw how good she was for my dad. Mainly because I bothered spending time with them, which my sister hadn't yet found it in herself to do.

That didn't mean we were best friends, or that I appreciated her giving me a look that meant she was onto me. Like we shared a secret. I only stuck my tongue out at her, the way I would've done to Darcy or Raina.

She smiled wide. I knew she loved it when she felt like we were getting along and I was accepting of her and their relationship. I did want to be. She was such a nice person, and it wasn't her fault there was such a wide age difference. She made Dad happy. That was all that mattered.

"I just happened to be the only person around who cared that he was in the hospital," I shrugged, popping a slice of pepperoni in my mouth. "I felt bad for him."

"A cute guy like that doesn't have a girlfriend?" Holly teased.

"He works too much. Too hard. And he takes his work very seriously. He needs this time off, and more balance in his life."

"He needs somebody who'll take care of him," Holly reasoned.

"I'm sure he does. I'll mention it to him if and when we see each other." I got to work setting the table, eager to get off the subject. "So how's everything with work? I almost never get the chance to hear about it, and I'm sorry. It seems like every time I come by, we're talking about me."

"We're both interested in you," she reminded me with a wink, joining me with a stack of napkins and silverware. "Work's going great. I just landed the job of helping restore the old Montbatten house—they're turning it into a museum of the entire town's history."

"No kidding! That's amazing! You know, I just found an old picture last night." I rubbed my arms to calm the goosebumps. "A young girl standing in front of that house. It was stuck in an old book at the store. Isn't it funny, you bringing that name up."

"That's eerie," she agreed. "I guess it's meant to be that I got this job. I'll take your discovery as a good omen."

"What sort of restoration has to be done? I never got the impression the house fell into ruin."

"No, it didn't, but the last owners were modern." She said the word like it was unfit for human ears. "I'd love to get my hands on them, but they're long gone. They moved overseas after gifting the house to the town. I have to replicate the house's style the way it was at the time it was built, at the turn of the twentieth century."

"Boy, I'd love to have enough money that I'd be able to gift a house to the town," I sighed.

"You and me both," Holly agreed as she finished setting things up.

"If you want that sorta life, don't bother getting yourself hooked up with that detective," Dad advised in his usual gruff way.

My cheeks flamed. "Dad! Jeez. Hooked up?"

"What? You don't think I know the lingo? You think your old man doesn't know things?" He carried the lasagna to the table and left it to sit on a trivet in the center. "I think there's a lot of things about me that might surprise you, young lady."

"Please, don't tell me all the things at once. My poor heart might not be able to take it." I took the bread from the oven, which Dad insisted on slicing because evidently I was incapable of handling a knife with a sprained wrist.

Meanwhile, I had no idea why dinner was happening at

all. Yes, it traditionally took place at that time of day, but not usually with my dad. Not when he requested it.

"So, what's going on with you?" I asked him, since coming out and asking why he wanted to have dinner would've been rude.

"The usual. Work. You know how it is."

I eyed him up and down. "Liar, liar."

"No, I'm not."

"Your pants are literally on fire. They're smoking right now." I waved a hand around to clear the invisible smoke.

"Honey, just tell her. I know you're dying to." Holly wiped her mouth with her napkin, and one look her way revealed an absolutely glowing smile. She was radiant—the girl was already pretty, but now she practically shone.

A funny feeling washed over me just then. Like something was off. She was beaming, Dad was grinning like a goof, and they were making lovey-dovey eyes at each other from across the table.

Engaged? No, Holly wasn't wearing a ring.

She also wasn't drinking wine, when she normally had a glass of red when we ate pasta.

Oh, jeez.

"Emma, sweetheart, this might come as a shock," Dad began, somehow managing to sound gruff while also grinning goofily. "We both hope you can come to share our happiness about this."

"Okay," I whispered. My appetite, which had been just about ravenous on sitting down, had started to wane. I felt like a little girl all of a sudden. Like I was shrinking in my chair. Pretty soon I'd need a telephone book to sit on. But

I didn't know if they even made telephone books anymore.

He took a deep breath, eyes still fixed on Holly. He then said the four little words I never would've expected otherwise. "We're having a baby."

Oh, boy. I let it wash over me for a minute, allowed it to sink in. Pretty soon I knew I was taking too long to express my reaction. Something about the pair of them staring at me, waiting, told me so.

"Wow," I breathed. "I mean, wow. This is… wow!"

"I don't want you to feel any sort of way about it," Holly was quick to assure me, reaching over and closing a hand over mine. "And if you're unhappy, I understand. I really do."

"Oh, no, no! I'm not unhappy. Really, I'm not." I looked at Dad to make sure he understood. "I'm sorry I didn't jump for joy. You deserve that. I was surprised, is all." I let out a laugh I knew sounded nervous, but it was the best I could do.

"We're very happy about it." And he looked happy. Happier than I'd seen him in a long time. "Can you believe it? I'm gonna be a father again. At my age."

"You'll do just as good a job as you did the first go-around. I know it." I got up and gave him a hug even though my heart wasn't entirely in it. I really was happy for him, very happy.

And for Holly, who didn't have any kids and looked like this was a dream coming true for her. She deserved my wholehearted support most of all. I pulled her from her chair and threw my arms around her. "How are you feeling?

When are you due?"

"I'm feeling great. A little tired, but good. The doctor wants me to take it easy, of course." She rolled her eyes with a dramatic sigh.

"We've talked about this," Dad muttered.

"Why do you have to take it easy?" I asked. "And if that's the case, why the heck did you go to all the trouble of cooking dinner? I'm cooking for you next time."

"I'll take you up on that," she smiled. "But no, it's just because this is considered a geriatric pregnancy since I'm over thirty-five."

"Ew." My nose wrinkled. "You'd think they'd come up with a nicer name. It makes you sound…"

"Ancient," she groaned. "It makes me sound ancient. I keep inspecting my face for wrinkles and age spots."

"Nothing wrong with either of those things," Dad muttered, examining the back of his hand.

I shrugged. "I guess they know what they're talking about, even if you don't have so much as a touch of grey in all the gorgeous hair."

"I color my hair," she admitted in a whisper.

"Oh. It's beautiful." There went my foot, falling out of my mouth as always. "Anyway, I don't normally say this, but he knows best and you should listen to him." I jerked a thumb in Dad's direction.

"Should I be glad to hear that?" Dad asked behind me.

We sat back down and I made a point of steering the conversation all over the baby front to keep the good vibes going. Holly was due on New Year's Eve, which of course I squealed over before we wondered whether she'd make it until midnight or have one of those babies that ends up on the news for being born moments after.

Meanwhile, inside? Inside, I was a mess. I couldn't help wondering what this would do to Mom. And Darcy. And how they'd find a way to take it out on me, being the messenger and all.

For one wild, panicked moment I considered not saying a word about it at all. But how long could I keep it from them in a town like Cape Hope? Someone would see her and tell Mom and that might be just as bad. If not worse.

She deserved to hear it from me.

Maybe after I took a six-month trip to Nepal or something.

CHAPTER THREE

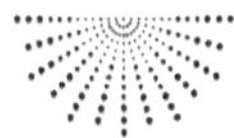

"And she's gonna die. I mean, she's really gonna die." I shoved a piece of bacon in my mouth without hardly tasting it. "Not before she kills me."

"Why would your mom kill you?" Joe asked, signaling the waitress for more coffee.

"Because Holly's pregnant. Duh." I rolled my eyes. "You know how it is. People are always trying to kill the messenger when it isn't the messenger's fault."

"I don't think it'll make her angry."

"I don't think you know my mother."

"I've spent time with her. Enough time that I can tell you she doesn't seem like the sort of woman who'd bite your head off just because somebody else is pregnant. I can't even imagine her being upset if you went to her tomorrow and announced a pregnancy."

"Are you kidding? She already has names picked out. *For my children.*"

"Exactly."

"But this isn't the same," I groaned. "This is her husband. Her husband of more than twenty years. He not only found a new girlfriend in, like, no time flat, but now she's pregnant. With his child," I hissed.

"Oh, thanks for the clarification. I was wondering if the baby was his."

"I'm starting to think you're not taking this seriously."

He shrugged. "Sorry. It's just that he's not her husband anymore."

"I know. But in her heart… It's not easy for a person to let go of such a long relationship. I wouldn't know—I mean, I do know. Sort of. But we're not talking twenty years."

"Oh? What's the story?" He folded his arms on the table. Strong arms. I remembered how they felt around me and wished I didn't.

"We don't need to talk about that."

"Sure, we do. You're the queen of asking prying questions. One might call it a talent. Or a curse."

I narrowed my eyes in what I hoped was a menacing manner. "I'm not sure I like this relaxed version of you. The one who smiles a lot more and says obnoxious things."

His head tipped to the side. "Do you have something in your eye?"

"Shut up." Another piece of bacon. "I found my fiancé cheating on me months ago. In our bed. In our apartment, which is now mine."

"Ouch. What a jerk."

"Thank you. No, it wasn't twenty years together, but it was painful. I've managed not to throw anything at the girl he was with, who by the way I see in town from time to time and yes, she stuck threatening notes under my wind-shield wipers—"

"What?"

"But it's okay. Still, if I saw her on the street and she looked pregnant, it would… it would hurt." I touched my chest before eating another piece of bacon. "It would hurt my heart."

"If you're worried about your heart, you should lay off the bacon."

"Hmm. Remember when I was the person who flew to your side when you were in the hospital? That was me, right? I asked you to come to breakfast so I could ask your advice."

For the first time since we'd met up, he didn't get sarcastic. He unfolded his arms, sitting up straight. "You're right. All this time off must be going to my head. I think you're right; this might hit your mom kinda hard. It'll be best for her to hear it from you, as much as you don't want to be the one to tell her."

Darn him. The sincerity in his voice mixed with the effect sunlight had on his ridiculous face—highlighting the dark stubble on his cheeks, turning his jade eyes into something closer to green fire—made my stomach go all fluttery.

I looked down at my plate, which was basically a pile of cholesterol and sugar. But those two things, even combined, were less dangerous than the sight of Joe Sullivan when he was being all tender and understanding.

"And there's my sister, too, and something tells me she'll be even harder to bring around." I stirred a bunch of eggs around with my fork. "She's never gotten over Dad finding somebody new, especially somebody so much younger than him."

"I can imagine that would be tough, too. And icky."

I snorted. "Icky? Yeah, that's a good word for it. She feels very icky about the whole thing. I just want everybody to get along. I want us to be a family."

"Things are never going to be the way they used to be. I know that's hard to accept. Maybe this is the new normal. This is the way things are now. Your sister needs to come around in her own time. Who knows? A new baby might be just what it takes."

"That's a lot of pressure for one baby."

"I think you'll all make it work. I've met both your parents, and they're good people. I'm an excellent judge of character."

"I guess that makes you good at your job." I took a mouthful of French toast.

"I guess so. I generally know when a person's bullshitting when I ask questions."

"Did you think I was when you interrogated me?"

"That wasn't an interrogation. How many times do I have to remind you of that?"

"Anyway, how are you feeling? What's going on with you? Are you more relaxed now?"

"I'm a lot more relaxed when I'm not with you," he informed me with an overly sweet smile.

"I guess I shouldn't have invited you out for breakfast."

"You invited me for breakfast—in a café rivaling your mother's, by the way, but I won't tell her that—"

"You will die!" I whispered.

"—so you could use me as a sounding board," he concluded. "Don't act like this was all out of the goodness of your heart."

Again, I stirred my eggs. "Maybe I wanted to check in with you. Make sure you're doing okay. You only had your attack a few days ago."

"I think those eggs are scrambled enough."

"Stirring them keeps me from throwing them in your smirking face. So." I continued to very deliberately stir while staring at him.

"Point taken. But thanks for caring. I know you do. I have a bad habit of being sarcastic when I don't know how to thank a person for being nice to me."

There was an awkward silence thanks to that. A change of subject was needed. And I had the perfect topic.

"Look at the neat picture I found." I bent, fishing around in my bag for the book. "It was at Darcy's shop. Who knows how old it is. I don't know who the girl is, but I wanna find out."

He leaned in to look at the photo which I placed on the table. "Hmm. Interesting. Nice house, too."

"It's one of the nicest houses in town, and was owned by one of the richest families. I can't stop thinking about her. I want to learn who she was."

"Why? She's probably just somebody from the family."

"I don't know. I can't explain it. Doesn't she look sad? Around the eyes, mostly?"

"She does, I guess."

"I wonder if she was ever happy again. You know? Like, did things change? Did her life pick up? Why was she so sad in the first place? The family died off ages ago. Why was she in front of the house, on the lawn? What was she doing there?"

"Landscaping?"

"You're a lot of help." I snatched it away and tucked it inside the book. "You clearly lack the sensitivity to appreciate this poor, pregnant girl's life."

"You don't know she was poor."

"I didn't mean it literally. And think about it: she's not wearing a ring and those were different times. This picture's at least sixty years old, maybe seventy. It wasn't smiled upon back then."

"True, but if she's a member of that rich family, she probably had a safety net. Her parents probably took care of her."

"Or," I countered, lowering my voice and my brow, "they sent her away. They banished her from the family along with her baby."

"If they wanted to get rid of her, they would've done it while she was pregnant. And then brought her back once the baby was born. Right? I'm not as up-to-speed as you clearly are on these things."

"Obviously."

"Doesn't that make sense, though? They wouldn't have let her hang around the house. In town. Where everybody would know the daughter of a wealthy family got pregnant outside marriage."

"I can't help but feel like you put a pin in my balloon and popped it."

"Why?" He laughed. "What's so wrong with that? Is this story only interesting if she was rich?"

"Drop it."

"No, I wanna know!"

"These eggs are still throwable."

He held up his hands, laughing. "Okay, fine. Truce. I don't feel like leaving here with egg on my face."

Which reminded me. "Oh, shoot, I have to go. I promised Mom I'd be in this morning. I kinda sorta might've told her we were hanging out." I signaled for the check, eyeing the clock.

"Because you knew she'd give you the okay if she thought we were spending time together?"

"What about it? I know how the woman thinks. She's completely focused on getting little Elinor and Frederick into the world."

"Who?"

"Those are they names she's picked out for my kids," I explained. "She's the world's biggest Jane Austen fan. Hence my name. And Darcy's."

His lips twitched.

"Shut it," I warned. "Is this in any way surprising, given my mother?"

"Not even a little bit," he admitted. "Let me know how it goes?"

I slid cash into the folder holding the receipt and got myself together. "Are you kidding? You'll probably hear about it on the news before I get the chance."

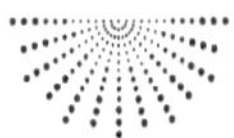

CHAPTER FOUR

"Sorry, sorry, sorry." I ran into the café carrying Lola under one arm. "I lost track of time."

Instead of chiding me for being late, Mom gasped in horror. "What's wrong with Lola?"

I stopped in my tracks so I could stare at the woman who brought me into the world. "I could've been in an accident that kept me from getting here when I said I'd be in, but you're more concerned about the dog?" I looked at Lola. She looked up at me and probably wondered when she'd get her next treat.

"You're carrying her!"

"Yes, I am. Because bless her heart, those short little legs don't help when I'm in a hurry." I set her up on her little doggy bed in the kitchen and tossed her a treat to keep her occupied before washing my hands and pulling back my long, blond hair. Blond hair that was awfully limp and lifeless. I wasn't one for the salon, not unless there was a special occasion happening, but I wondered if a trip wasn't in store.

It had nothing to do with the presence of both Deke and Joe. Nothing whatsoever.

"How was your morning rendezvous?" Mom asked in way too loud a voice as I slid behind her to take the other register. As always, the café was packed at this time of the morning. Especially in summer, when visitors to the town's many bed and breakfasts were having a stroll.

I happened to meet Mrs. Merriweather's eyes and noticed how they danced. For a woman in her eighties, she still had quite the fire blazing in her furnace. "It wasn't a rendezvous," I whispered, shaking my head. I knew she could hear me, thanks to her ultrasensitive hearing aid.

"No need to tell me, Emma," she winked under her latest confection of a hat. Wide-brimmed, with a wide blue sash which wrapped around the crown before coming down on either side, so she could tie a festive bow under her chin. "It's been a long time since my last rendezvous, but I remember well how it goes."

Oh, boy. I didn't know whether to smile and let the moment pass or ask for more details because, honestly, who wouldn't? And something told me she'd be all too happy to share. Loudly.

It was best to let it go. People were trying to eat— including children who didn't need to hear about how things were done in Mrs. Merriweather's day. "Okay, here's your bran muffin and tea," I said before waving the next customer forward.

"I was starting to think you overslept, Emma," Mr. Hutchins barked in his usual way.

"Me? Never! You know how it is. You spend years

waking up before dawn to keep the drill sergeant off your back…" I jerked my head toward Mom. "It becomes a habit."

The old Marine laughed heartily at this. "I only wish my drill sergeants had been as sweet and lovely as this one. More boys would've enlisted."

"Oh, you." Mom blushed, waving a hand.

"Don't let the sweetness fool you," I warned. "She's a real taskmaster under that smile and those dimples." Yes, yes, get Mom in a super good mood before bringing her world crashing down around her. Great thinking.

Maybe she'd take it well. A lot of water had passed under the bridge since the divorce. Business was better than ever, she had a lot of great friends who'd kill for her. She had plenty of life left in her, too. There was no reason she couldn't find a man in her fifties, for heaven's sake.

She was devoted to the café, though. *Sweet Nothings* had already been a huge part of her life even when she was married and raising two girls. Now that the marriage was no more and her girls were grown? It meant everything.

Whoever she found would need to have a lot of patience regarding her work schedule.

Or maybe, just maybe, she'd need to take a step back and loosen her death grip on the reins.

"You know," I murmured once Mr. Hutchins had stepped away, "he has a point."

"What point?" she chuckled.

"You're too pretty and have too nice a nature to be stuck behind the counter all day."

"Where do you think I should go? To the kitchen?"

"You know what I mean." I turned away from the

register to brew espresso for a cappuccino. "You need to live a little. Get out more. Meet new people."

"Like I don't already know enough people."

"Mom."

"Emma." She shot me a weary look. "Please, let's not get into the conversation about my working too hard. You know who you sound like."

And this was not the time to turn the conversation around to my father, who was exactly who she was thinking of then. Smooth move on my part. "You devote so much time to my happiness, and Darcy's. Since when is it a crime to want you to be happy, too?"

"I'm happy. I am!" she insisted when I rolled my eyes. "This is my dream. Running this café. It's like the hub of the town, have you ever noticed? Not to pat myself on the back..."

"Pat away," I urged. "You deserve the credit."

"It's where people gather. They come in, they feel like they're visiting friends. That means everything."

"I completely agree. But Mom, it's not everything. Not completely. I want you to have fun, too!"

"I have fun. This is fun!" Her wide smile hardened when she splashed coffee on her apron. "See? Fun."

"Oh, so much fun," I agreed, shaking my head. She was incorrigible. A hopeless romantic who all but thrust her daughters toward the nearest men, yet she couldn't find it in herself to try again.

"You should try online dating." That came from Mrs. Dudley, one of the teachers at the local elementary school. She was my first-grade teacher, which even all these years later made it weird for me to serve her and have an adult conversation.

I mean, I once had an accident in the middle of a hand-writing lesson. Not the sort of thing I liked to remember, but it always came rushing back whenever I saw her.

Mom scoffed at this. "No way! I wouldn't know the first thing about it. And who would want to get involved with a woman who only spends a few hours a day away from work?"

"Which is why you should also hire extra people to cover shifts," I suggested. "So you can step away sometimes, take a breather."

She shook her adamant little head. "I can't imagine it. What in the world would I do?"

"Live?" I suggested. "Have fun? Get a life—no offense?" I squeaked when Mom turned to glare my way.

"This is my life. I like it just fine the way it is. And unless you'd like to have a fight over this, young lady, I suggest we change the subject."

I exchanged a look with Mrs. Dudley which very clearly said it was time to let things go. I knew what it meant when Mom's bottom teeth jutted out like a bulldog's.

"Okay. Let's change the subject," I agreed as I reached into the bakery case to pull out a blueberry muffin for Mrs. Dudley.

As it turned out, I didn't have to be the one to change it.

The door flung open—like, literally burst open so hard the bell clanged instead of chiming merrily—framing my Auntie Nell and her stormy face and her clenched fists and her general air of wanting to murder somebody.

Funny thing, but I had the feeling I knew what had her so upset. Short of vaulting over the counter, knocking down a few geriatrics and maybe breaking their hips, there was nothing I could do to stop her or keep her outside.

"Hey, Mom, can you... go do something in the kitchen? Lola might need something," I suggested, staring across the room with roughly the same amount of horror as someone watching a funnel cloud bearing down on them. So I imagined, anyway.

It was too late. Certain disasters were unavoidable, it seemed.

"Nell? What's the matter?" my poor, innocent mother called out.

"You don't know?" Nell gasped as she worked her way through the waiting customers. "Oh, Sylvia."

"Maybe let's not talk about this now?" I suggested with a smile tight enough to crack my teeth. "Maybe this isn't the time or place?"

"This is something you know about?" Mom asked. The poor woman was so confused, her head kept swinging back and forth between Nell and me.

I couldn't have begged Nell any harder with my eyes. If I'd dropped to my knees with my folded hands raised, I didn't think I could get my point across any better.

"Um, yeah. I think. Granted, I don't know what Nell has in mind, but I think I have a pretty good idea? And I think maaaaaybe it doesn't need to be shared right here and now? In the café? With all these people around?" I shrugged.

Maybe I could pull the fire alarm, and everybody would leave.

"Emma makes a good point. I thought you knew." Nell's face fell. "I guess it's best to learn these things from a loved one."

"Wow, never would've considered that," I muttered under my breath.

"We can go to the kitchen," Mom suggested, casting a look my way as she led Nell back there.

Leaving me with a café full of customers, all of whom wondered what the heck was going on. Something told me they'd know all too well before long. I put on as genuine a smile as possible and continued with my work.

Before something crashed in the kitchen and poor, traumatized Lola came flying out like somebody shot her out of a cannon.

"Oh, honey!" I gasped, bending to pick her up. "I'm sorry."

"Is everything okay back there?" one of the unfamiliar tourists asked. "And do you typically handle a dog here in the café?"

Dang it.

"I'll put her back in her bed and wash my hands and be right back out. Please, excuse me. This is a very… strange day." I practically fled to the kitchen, where the sight of an overturned prep bowl greeted me on entrance.

And beyond that, my mother. Standing with her hands covering her face.

Nell looked like she wished she'd never left the house that morning. "I'm sorry," she mouthed over Mom's shoulder as she gave her a hug.

"Maybe you should take her home. Hey, Mom." I rubbed

her back in passing. "Why don't you go home for a while? Or, all day. Whatever the case may be. I've got things under control here."

"I never thought…" Mom mumbled from behind her hands. "I never imagined this." I had to turn away. It was too much. I knew this would happen, but I couldn't imagine how it would hurt to watch it happen.

"I'll take her home," Nell whispered, and all I could do was nod. I had to get back out to the register, where people were still waiting to be helped. Or so I hoped, after the drama they'd just witnessed.

"Clean hands!" I announced, holding them up as I emerged from the kitchen. "Washed 'em twice. Let's get some sugar and caffeine up in our faces, folks!"

"Is your mother all right?" Mrs. Merriweather asked from her chair against the wall.

"She's fine. But she'll be taking some much-needed time off today. She works endlessly, you know?"

"Does it have to do with the baby?"

I almost dropped a scone on the floor. The room went quiet, and more than a few pairs of eyes settled on me. And my stomach.

"It's not mine," I hissed, glaring.

So, word had spread. Fabulous. I should've known, obviously, having lived in the town all my life. News spread like a rash around there. And just about everybody was willing to be a carrier.

Which meant.

Oh, no.

Moments later, the door opened rather violently once

again. This time, a girl who looked a lot like me entered the café with red-rimmed eyes and cut straight through the crowd, going to the kitchen. Once again, quite a few people looked around in confusion.

"Does this happen a lot?" one random person asked another.

"Excuse me. I'm sorry. I really am." I cringed hard enough to hurt before dashing to the kitchen.

Where Darcy was on the floor, cuddling Lola while crying into her fur.

"Oh, Darce," I whispered. She didn't look up.

"Hey, anybody work here?"

I leaned back through the doorway and was about to ask the customer to have just a tiny bit more patience, that I'd be with them in just a second, when it became clear this wasn't just any old customer.

It was a customer who looked a lot like Deke Bellingham, who wore a familiar smile as he slid familiar sunglasses away from his familiar face.

He jerked a thumb toward the door. "A bunch of people left as I was coming in. They didn't seem happy. What's going on?"

He had a bad habit of asking questions like that.

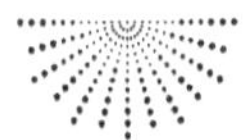

CHAPTER FIVE

"And that's why the whole world was falling apart at exactly the moment you walked into the café today." I lifted my wineglass and tilted it Deke's way before raising it to my lips. Yes, wine was just what this day called for.

Deke blinked hard. "Oh. Wow. That's a lot."

"And lucky you, happening to walk in as disgruntled customers left in a huff." Maybe I needed another glass.

"It wasn't that many. And they were probably tourists, anyway."

"Tourists who leave reviews."

"I don't think your mom's café needs to rely on reviews."

"No, I guess you're right," I admitted. "But it doesn't help, either."

He sighed while leaning forward, reaching across the table to close a hand over my good wrist. It wasn't exactly unlike him to be physical—we'd kissed, and it was amazing —but we hadn't spent a ton of time together, either, thanks to his wacky schedule conflicting with mine.

His touch was welcome. Just… different. Something I could see myself getting used to.

"You can't take everybody's problems on your shoulders." His smile was warm, caring, and utterly necessary just then. "Frankly, I think it was wrong of your Aunt Nell to barge in while there were customers and lay something like that on your mom."

"You know, I was thinking the same thing," I admitted. "It's not like her to be so thoughtless. How did she think Mom was going to react? Obviously, she'd be stricken."

"You should take it up with her."

I pulled my hand back, aghast. "Oh, I don't wanna start a fight."

"It doesn't have to be a fight," he reasoned. "You're an adult. You're not a little kid. You don't have to, I don't know, defer to people just because they're older than you. This is your mom, your family. I know your Aunt Nell is very close to family, but it isn't her name that'll be dragged around because of this."

"You make a good point." I wasn't just saying that, either. He had a way of getting me to relax. My breathing slowed, my shoulders loosened. "It's always been sort of a joke, you know? The way people gossip in town. The café is gossip central. But that isn't always appropriate."

"Maybe it's time to let people know how inappropriate it can be," he suggested in a soft voice.

"Not maybe. Definitely." I could smile for real now. "Thank you."

"No problem. See? I knew there was a reason this was the exact week I was planning to visit. So, how's it feel?"

"How's what feel? Having you here? It's pretty nice."

"Thank you, but not what I was talking about."

My cheeks flamed. I hoped the dim lighting in the restaurant was enough to hide it. "Oh. What were you talking about?"

"Being a big sister! You've been the little sister your whole life. Now, you'll be the one somebody looks up to, and oh, gee, I almost feel sorry for the kid."

"I sure have missed your sense of humor. It's such a delight."

"You know I don't mean it."

"I have my doubts sometimes."

"Well, I don't. I was only kidding around. So? What do you think about the baby coming? You've spent the salad and appetizer courses telling me how your mom broke down and how Darcy practically drowned Lola in tears. What do you think? How do you feel?"

There was something about his probing gaze. It left me wanting to open up, totally and completely, and that was a dangerous impulse. Deke was a great guy who, for some strange reason, I couldn't help but feel attracted to.

The reason wasn't so strange. When I stopped putting up barriers between us, it was obvious he was the whole package. A little flighty when it came to some things. When he was in his zone, there was no interrupting him for anything.

Not even for common courtesy. I'd learned that one the hard way.

Otherwise, he was great. Supportive, a calm head in a crisis. Hot. Pretty darn hot. The light linen suit he wore for our dinner date was a departure from his usual jeans and button-down shirt, but I was liking it on him.

One thing would never change. His penchant for leaving the top two buttons of his shirt undone. I didn't know what I'd do if I ever saw him in a tie.

He was waiting for me to answer, waiting with patience and kindness and genuine interest. I only wished I knew what to say.

"I guess I'm happy about the baby. Dad is thrilled, like over the moon excited. And this is Holly's first baby, so she's very excited, too. But since she's over thirty-five, the doctor is concerned—"

"Hang on a sec. I'm glad your dad is happy, and I'm happy for Holly. But I didn't ask about them, with all due respect. I asked about you. You have a tendency to absorb other people's emotions and talk about them like they're your own."

This slammed me back in my chair. "Wow. That sounds terrible."

"It's not terrible! You're a good person. A good, kind person."

"You made it sound like I'm some co-dependent loser."

"Emma..." His eyes slid closed. "I meant nothing like that. I only want to know how you feel. What you're thinking. Not in relation to your parents or your sister or anybody else. Just you. How do you feel about this new addition to your family?"

I resisted the impulse to squirm in the chair. The fact was, his questions made me acutely uncomfortable. This was always going to be a thorn for us, I suspected, the way he made me look at myself even when I didn't particularly want to.

Was he right about me?

He had to be, since it was way too much of a challenge, coming up with something to say that came only from me. "Uh, well, I love babies. I look forward to taking care of him or her."

"That's a start," he grinned.

"I know Holly will make a good mother, and I already know how good Dad is at that sort of thing. So I'm not worried about what the baby will be born into."

"Good to hear."

"I do wish Darcy would come around, and no, this isn't about her. I want the baby to feel loved."

"I'm sure it will, even if one of its older sisters isn't super enthused."

"I guess." The more I thought about it, the deeper my discomfort. "I might be a little jealous."

"Jealous?" His eyebrows shot up. "Of who? Holly? This is a left turn."

"No, not of Holly. Of the baby. It's so weird." I decided to look out the window at the brilliant sunset over the bay.

"Why, Emma?"

"It's dumb. I feel so stupid for even saying that." I waved a hand, still looking away.

"I really do want to know. Not to make you feel bad, but to see if I can help you feel better. You know you can trust me, right?"

Trust. What a funny word. I used to think I could trust a man, and look where that got me. Though life had hardly turned out badly, I was still timid when it came to trust. "I envy the baby because it will get more time with Dad, I think. If it weren't for the baby, he wouldn't want to retire. He'd probably work until his last breath. Now? He has a reason to step back, collect his pension, and spend his time with this new person. And that sorta sucks, to be blunt."

"You didn't get that time with him."

"Not really. We were mostly with Mom, at the café. He could hardly take us out on ride-alongs."

Deke snorted. "Understood."

"It's selfish and immature, and I know it. I'm not proud of myself."

"You don't have to rake yourself over the coals for this, you know. Anybody would feel the same way about a second family. I know I did."

Our entrees came then, just when I was ready to demand he tell me more. Instead, I had to play nice and be polite to the server. The scent of grilled shrimp and scallops combined with roasted garlic and butter, making my mouth water.

There were more important things to worry about just then. "What do you mean, you did?" I asked the moment we were alone again.

He lifted his fork and knife, set on tearing into his steak. "I mean, I have younger siblings. Much younger. Just like you, my father had a second family after divorcing my mom. There's my sister, who you spoke to on the phone."

I had to look down at this. Yes, I'd spoken to her, and I'd thought she was Deke's girlfriend before he explained the situation.

"I also have a younger full brother. Besides them, I have a half-brother and half-sister who are both in their preteens."

"You never told me that!"

"You never asked." He winked before taking his first bite. His eyes rolled back a bit, and a groan escaped. "Oh, my God."

"I told you, they have some of the best food in town. Though I can't imagine why you'd choose steak when you have the entire ocean to choose from."

"I'll be here all week, remember. Let me pace myself."

I twirled fettuccine around my fork. "So, you didn't totally love the idea of a second family?"

"Not especially. I shared some of the feelings you have, too. About another set of kids getting the attention and affection we didn't get a lot of while we were growing up. Topher, my younger brother, was barely out of braces when our parents divorced. He could've used Dad then, a male figure to look up to. Dad, meanwhile, was flying out to France all the time to see his mother—the one who recently passed—and that was where he met his current wife. They live in Manhattan now."

I bit my tongue rather than ask why Deke had to be the one to settle the estate when his father was still alive and well. It could've been too painful for him, I reasoned.

"These things are always complicated, so you don't have to put yourself down for being human and feeling the way so many people do when they're faced with this. Okay?"

"Okay." Strange how my appetite came roaring back after that. I dug into my seafood with a lot more vigor than before.

"What else is going on? Since all we've talked about is your upcoming baby brother or sister?"

"I think I found a mystery to solve."

"Oh, boy. I think I just lost my appetite."

"Come on. Give me a little credit. Like a smidge." I held my thumb and forefinger less than an inch apart. "It's nothing dangerous."

"So you always say…"

I rolled my eyes. "Anyway, I thought it could be a fun thing to get Darcy's help with, now that she's sorta down about the baby."

"Hmm. I know you wouldn't deliberately bring your sister into something that could spell potential danger, so maybe this won't end in near-tragedy."

"Why does everybody think I actively seek out opportunities to get myself killed?" I asked the ceiling, which had no answer.

"It sure seems like you do."

"I don't! As I said, this isn't anything dangerous. I found an old picture. Wanna see?"

"Sure," he agreed in a tone that felt a little too indulgent. Like he was throwing me a bone.

"You don't have to sound so excited," I grumbled as I reached for my purse.

"Sorry. I don't give a random, old picture the full treatment. Have we met?"

I sighed without offering a response because he was right. I shouldn't have expected anything else. He knocked me over not a few minutes after we met because he was too busy getting a good shot and either forgot I was standing there or didn't care much.

"Fine, fine." I pulled out the photo and placed it in front of him.

"Can I ask a question?"

"Better than anybody I know."

He snickered. "Why do you carry it around with you. Are you related?"

"I can't explain why I carry it around. I see her and I feel… I don't know. Connected, somehow. I know it sounds lame."

"Not lame at all. I was only curious."

"You have a way of making curiosity sound like criticism. Anybody ever tell you that?"

"Anybody ever tell you how you manage to take curiosity as criticism nine times out of ten?"

"It's that eyebrow." I pointed. "It arches. I can always tell what you're thinking. You need to Botox that bad boy if you plan on passing yourself off as just a concerned, nice guy."

"I'll take that under consideration." He chuckled. He seemed endlessly patient tonight. I remembered he was on vacation and maybe not in the mood for snarky banter.

Turning his attention back to the photo, he cocked his head to the side. "Isn't that the Montbatten house?"

"You're familiar with it?"

"Aside from the fact that it's a perfect example of seaside Victorian architecture, my distant relatives were close to the Montbattens in their day. I feel like there's a picture of my great-grandmother playing on the front lawn when she couldn't have been more than five years old."

"How neat! Do you recognize this girl?"

My heart sank when he shook his head, though I couldn't imagine why I expected him to know her. He said it was his distant relatives, didn't he? "No, I don't. The family died out, didn't they?"

"Yeah, the last surviving daughter died not long ago. The house was purchased by some tacky couple—hey, Holly said so," I added to defend myself when he looked up with that eyebrow quirking again. "Now, it belongs to the town. It's a wonder the old lady didn't put that in her will."

"Some people don't think of things like that by the time a will comes along," Deke mused. "This can't be her, then. She never had kids. That much I remember. Millicent, right?"

"Right."

"Hmm. Maybe it's a cousin, or a family friend."

"I found it in an old book donated to Darcy years ago, when she first opened the store. I'm fascinated by it. I don't know why."

"Because you have such a vibrant imagination. And you're deeply empathetic. You feel for people. Even people who aren't alive anymore, whose names you don't know."

"I guess." I shrugged as I put the picture away. It was more than that. I wished I could put a finger on it.

"Can I offer you two any dessert?" the server asked with a hopeful smile. "Coffee? Tea?"

It was like another person's voice came out of my mouth when I answered. "I'm okay, thanks."

Deke held onto the table like he was afraid he'd fall off his chair otherwise. "Are you serious? No dessert?"

"Could you not?" I asked through a tight smile. "You're free to do whatever you want, of course."

"No, thanks. I'm stuffed," he told the server before turning back to me. "I'm worried about you."

"You make me sound like a glutton."

"I know you like your sweets. You're still upset."

"Deke… I'm sorry." I slumped back in my chair, helpless. "I am upset. For Mom. And worried about her. Here I am, out with you—and I'm so glad to be with you—while she's at home. Probably still hurting."

"You should go to her," he suggested.

"But we're out together!"

"Your heart is with her. It's okay, I have all week. Remember? Can I walk you to her house?"

"Please." I leaned in, taking his hand. "Thank you. You're too understanding."

"You're right." He winked. "It's part of my charm."

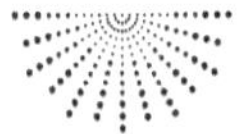

CHAPTER SIX

It was a blessedly dry night with hardly a touch of humidity in the air for the first time in ages. For once, I wasn't wasting my time when I did my hair for a night out.

"It's so weird," I mused as we walked. "I feel… pleasantly full. Satisfied. Not stuffed."

"You realize that's because you didn't eat dessert, right?"

"Don't judge me," I warned.

"I'm not. If anything, I'm honored to be here while you're reaching this deep understanding. It's like watching a kid learn to balance on a bike for the first time."

"It's been a while since I've wanted to hit you." I sighed. "I was honestly hoping we'd turned a corner."

He reached for my hand, and I didn't pull away. "Maybe I should keep at least one hand still, then, so you can't use it as a weapon."

"I've got a pretty strong grip, so don't get too full of yourself." I squeezed to prove my point. "I've spent my life stirring thick batters and carrying heavy pans and trays. Just sayin'."

"That's a pretty firm grip," he admitted. "My father always said a firm handshake is the mark of a worthwhile person. Somebody you can trust. He only did business with people whose handshakes were firm."

"Does he know you carry so much of his wisdom with you now?"

His smile slipped. "He died a while back."

"Oh. Deke." I slowed, then stopped. Being attached to me the way he was, he had no choice but to stop along with me. "I had no idea. You never talked about it." No wonder he had to settle his grandmother's estate in his father's place. He said they lived in Manhattan, and I'd assumed he meant his dad. He was talking about his stepmother and her kids.

"I mean, when was the right time to bring up something like that?" he asked with a shrug. "Come on. Let's keep walking. It's a beautiful night."

It really was. Rows and rows of Victorian homes were lit thanks to the old-fashioned gaslights lining the streets. Most of them were used as boutiques, art galleries, bed and breakfasts. People sat on porches, rocking slowly, enjoying drinks and laughing softly.

"It's idyllic," he murmured with a smile. "I really like it here. You're lucky to have grown up in the middle of it all."

My heart swelled with pride. "I know I am. It's one of those things where I know I could take it for granted, but I don't. If I'm meant to have roots, I'm glad they're here."

"And you get to see people you know wherever you go."

"That's true." I looked at him, waiting to see what

brought that up, and found that his eyebrows had somehow grown together over his nose. Just one single line.

It didn't take long to figure out why. Coming toward us was a couple holding hands the way we were. And the red-headed, pick-skirted female half of the pair looked awfully familiar. And awfully upset when our eyes met.

"For the record, most people around here don't look like they're gonna cry when they see me," I murmured as we continued on. What choice did I have? I wasn't going to cross the street after seeing Nell.

Especially not with so many people watching. Wasn't I just saying how much I loved my home?

Rather than introduce me to the stranger whose hand she held, she rushed my way. "Emma. I was so wrong. I don't know how I'll ever forgive myself."

I accepted her almost violent hug with a sigh. "It's okay. I mean, it's not strictly okay. I was planning on waiting to talk to her when we were alone, but I should've known better. Somebody was bound to spill the beans."

"I could've been much smarter about it," she sniffled, pulling away. "I feel so terrible. It was bad enough when the problem was just the baby, but now…"

"She was always going to hurt because of this," I shrugged. "But yeah, it could've been timed better. I guess anybody else could just as easily have come in and asked how she felt about Dad's new baby."

"So long as you're not angry with me."

"I'm not angry," I whispered. "So don't worry about it."

The man behind her cleared his throat. "Nell…"

"Oh!" Her eyes lit up. "Sorry, Rance. Didn't mean to forget about you."

Rance? I looked him up and down. Very attractive, probably in his sixties, fit like he took care of himself. A thick head of salt-and-pepper hair. "I'm Emma Harmon."

"Sylvia's younger daughter," Nell explained. "This is Rance Peabody. He's new in town. Comes into the library all the time."

"She finally noticed me." He grinned, shaking my hand. Nice grip, strong handshake. "Nell talks about you and your sister all the time."

"The closest thing to daughters I've ever had." She beamed. "And you're Deke, right? It's good to see you again."

"The same goes double." He shook Rance's hand and seemed impressed. "What are you two up to this evening?"

No doubt, Nell blushed. She might as well have been a girl half her age or younger, practically giggling over her new beau. "We were going for ice cream cones."

Now, if I were my Auntie Nell, I would've invited Deke and myself to join them. I would've bulldozed my way into the situation. It occurred to me that this might be the perfect opportunity to turn the tables. Give her a taste of her own medicine.

"That sounds like fun."

"What about you two?" she asked with a knowing smile. Oh, terrific. Now that she had a gentleman in her life, she'd be even more determined to get me hooked up with somebody.

"We're coming back from dinner," Deke ever-so-helpfully explained.

"Oh? Dinner for two? That's nice."

"Well, there are two of us…" I muttered.

Deke elbowed me. I elbowed him back.

Time to change the subject. "Hey, do you have lots of resources at the library where I could learn about family trees? The more famous, wealthy families in the area."

"Sure. You could go to the historical society, too, but I think they're busy working on the new museum. Either way, your face is always welcome at the library."

"Are you a student of history?" Rance asked. "I was a history professor in a former life, before I retired."

"How interesting." They'd make a great match. "I've always been interested in history, especially the town's, but this is specific to a photo I found. I'd love to know who was in the picture. Maybe I can get it back to them somehow."

"Always thinking of other people," Nell practically cooed.

I stopped short of suggesting she tone it down a little. Loving and devoted was one thing, but she was a second away from licking her thumb and wiping the corner of my mouth.

"I guess I'll see you tomorrow. I don't want to hold you two up." Rance looked grateful. He was just trying to get his groove on with a new lady and didn't want two whipper-snappers getting in the way.

Though I doubted he thought of us as whippersnappers. He wasn't old enough for that.

"Hmm. I wonder what your mom would think of that." Deke snickered once there was enough distance between us after we'd parted ways.

"Of Nell dating somebody who looks and acts like he just, I don't know, rode a horse or played a game of tennis or something?"

"What?" he laughed.

"You know. One of those people who just exudes energy. Vitality. I've always wanted to be one of those people."

"I'd remind you the sugar in your diet is probably holding you back, but you'd only threaten to smack me."

"Yet you said it anyway."

"Yet I did." He took my hand again. "And you're not a sloth, Emma. You're one of the most energetic people I know. I can barely keep up with you."

I took the compliment without argument, too busy reflecting on Mom and Nell. "It's very nice for her, having somebody to date. Right now, I don't think my mom would be too thrilled. Don't get me wrong, she wants her friends to be happy. She wants everybody to be happy. That's the whole reason why she's such pain in the butt sometimes. She wants everybody to have what they want, what they need. And nobody can ever fault her for that."

"I would never dream of it," Deke murmured.

"But right now? I don't think her heart would be in any happy reaction. If anything, it'll feel like salt in the wound. I keep trying to convince her to put herself out there again."

"Ouch. That's a lot to ask of a person. Some people can get back up on the horse with no trouble. Others, it takes time. Some people never remarry after a divorce or death. My mother never has. She very rarely dates. And when she does, it's always in a friendly sort of way, not romantic. You know, like if she needs somebody to go with her to an event.

She'll have a date, but he'll be more of a friend than anything else. It's what makes her comfortable. I would never urge her to do anything that made her uncomfortable."

"I don't want to make my mom uncomfortable, either. I just want her to be happy."

"You mean the way she just wants you to be happy?" he asked, and I had the sense he was teasing. "You don't like it very much when she gets into your personal life and tries to tell you how to run it, do you?"

"You know I don't," I muttered.

"I'm sure it's the same for her, if not worse. Just, you know. Keep it in mind. When she's ready, she'll do what she has to do. Only she knows what that is."

"You're right. You're absolutely right." I smirked up at him. "How's it feel?"

"How does what feel?"

"Being right for once." We stopped in front of Mom's house. "This is it."

He looked it over with an approving expression. "Beautiful. Just the sort of house I would imagine you growing up in. The gingerbread trim, the big porch, the flowers growing out front."

"Don't forget the white picket fence," I teased. "It's the whole package."

"Hmm. The whole package. That sounds familiar." He was smiling in a funny sort of way as he bent to kiss my cheek. "Can I get a rain check on our date?"

"Absolutely." A tingle ran all through me from just the simplest little kiss. "And thank you. I know I tease you a lot, and we butt heads, but I really am glad you're here. And I'm so grateful to you for being so understanding."

"No problem. And if you need any help solving your mystery, let me know. I love that historical stuff, too." Another kiss, this one on the back of my hand, before he backed away and started walking down the street toward the house he was staying in for the week. I knew it well, having walked past it nearly every single day of my life.

It wasn't hard to imagine Miss Evesham, the mousy owner, being head-over-heels in love with him.

There was still a light burning in the living room, a light that reminded me of other matters that needed tending to. Instead of chasing after Deke and throwing my arms around him, the way impulse told me I should, I opened the gate and walked up the brick path to the front stairs.

CHAPTER SEVEN

"I'm not a child." Mom accepted the cup of tea I'd just brewed with a grateful smile. "I knew this would happen—or that it was possible, rather. Just like it's possible he'll marry her. I don't doubt that will happen someday, especially now with a baby."

I sat next to her with a tissue box between us and did my best to stay quiet, to let her talk it out without my interference.

"It's one thing to know something is possible," she sighed. "And another to have that something happen. I don't know why I'm so upset." She pulled a tissue from the box and dabbed at her eyes.

"It's understandable," I whispered.

"Is it, though? We've been apart for so long. He's moved on, and I knew he had. How could I not?" she chuckled. "It's in my face all the time. I see them together and it's not as painful as it was at first, but it still hurts."

"I didn't know you saw them together."

"How could I not? There's only so much square mileage in this town. Just because I don't talk about it doesn't mean it never happens."

"I didn't think. I'm sorry."

"No, no. You have nothing to be sorry about. Don't apologize." She took a long sip of tea before sighing. "It isn't as if I thought we'd ever get back together. Believe me, some things are best left where they are. But this…"

"Makes it real," I murmured.

"Yes. There's no going back from this. He's starting a new family, for heaven's sake. Not just shacking up with a girl practically young enough to be his daughter. They're going to be parents together."

I rested my head on her shoulder. "I know. It's a whole new thing. I didn't know what to think about it when I heard."

"You already knew, didn't you?"

I stiffened. "Yeeeeah? I mean, just since last night. I wanted to wait to tell you. Privately. Along with Darcy. I didn't mean to hurt you."

Another sigh. "You didn't. I wondered where all that talk about me dating came from."

"It wasn't just because of the baby," I was quick to say. "And it wasn't just dating we were talking about, either. You've worked so hard for so long. I know you're proud of what you've built. I'm proud of you. You're my hero."

"Stop," she scoffed.

"You are. I'm not just saying it." I pulled back to look critically at her. "You didn't know that? Do I not say it enough?"

"I don't think you've ever said it before. I'm silly Mom. Flighty. Always butting in."

"Mom, no. I mean… sometimes, yeah, with the butting in," I admitted. "But it's done out of love, and even my exasperation is loving, because I know your heart is in the right place. Otherwise? You're a warrior. You built that business from nothing. While raising us. And teaching us about work ethic and the finer points of running a business from the office. Not to mention how to make everybody feel welcome and at home in the process. You've done it with grace. Not everybody could've done that."

"You're going to make me cry again," she warned with a shaky laugh.

"You need to hear it. I'll tell you every single day if that's what it takes. You're incredible. You've got the biggest heart of anybody I know." I tucked a few stray strands of honey-blond hair behind her ear. It wasn't like her to look so disheveled, but she'd had a real day.

"How is your sister taking it?" she asked, looking down into her tea with a frown. "I called her earlier, but she didn't answer."

"She's upset. I knew she would be. I really didn't want either of you to find out this way."

"I know. These things happen. I guess she'll get over it." Her eyes cut my way. "It would be nice if she could enjoy having a little brother or sister. I don't want to deprive either of you of that experience. I hope she doesn't feel like she has to shut the baby out on my account."

"You'll have to talk to her about that. I think she needs to hear it from you." I leaned over to pull my phone from my purse, resting on the floor at my feet. She hadn't called or texted, not even to reply to any of my messages. Maybe she was with Karl. I hoped so.

"What's that?" Mom asked, noticing the photo at the top of the pile of junk in my bag. I needed to clean it out, but it always filled right back up again.

"Oh, I didn't show it to you?" I didn't think she was genuinely interested, but there had to be a shift in the conversation at some point. "I found it in one of Darcy's used books. Isn't it neat?"

"She's pretty," Mom murmured, though a frown washed over her face for a second. Naturally, it was a picture of a pregnant girl. That was bound to set her off.

But that wasn't what made her frown, as it turned out. "She looks a little like Millicent Montbatten. The nose, especially, and the little cleft in her chin. It's barely notice-able, but it's there. I can see her looking this way when she was a girl."

"She never had children, though. And she wasn't married, was she?"

"Not that I know of." She looked up at me. "Why are you carrying it in your purse?"

"I don't know. I felt drawn to the book the picture was tucked into, and I feel drawn to her. It's weird. I want to know who she was, and why she looks so sad."

"You think she looks sad? Hmm."

"You don't?"

"No. Wistful, maybe. Maybe she has regrets. But her eyes aren't sad. They're… determined. She's a strong girl, whoever this is." Mom shivered a little, then laughed at herself. "I guess I feel the same way about her as you do!"

"I'm going to the library tomorrow to research a little, specifically pertaining to that family. Now that you pointed out the resemblance, I'm obsessed with finding out if that's Millicent. What a scandal that would've been, huh?"

"If there was a scandal, I never heard about it."

"I think this would've been a little before your time, wouldn't it?"

"Ah, you're sweet," she laughed. "And actually, yes. I would've been a baby, if that."

I nudged her. "Hey! Maybe you're really her daughter! And you're actually an heiress!"

"Please," she said with a roll of her eyes. "You remember your grandparents. I was my mother's mirror image."

"True. Besides, I doubt there's any money left in the family. I wonder what Millicent did with her fortune."

"It's funny you mention that. There was a lot of speculation about what happened to her money after she died. You were away at school then. It was all people could talk about for days. Where was it? What had she done with it? There was no public reading of the will or anything like that. With no relatives in sight, who did it go to?"

Though I reminded myself that I was there for Mom's sake and that I should be comforting her, a buzzing sensation started in my head. Like a hive of bees had been overturned and the little suckers were going crazy.

What if it was Millicent in that picture? What if she had a baby out of wedlock back when that sort of thing was deeply frowned upon, especially in an old-money family like hers?

What if she'd left her wealth to her child?

It was silly. I shook my head, rising from the couch, determined to get my sweet fix on. "Do you have anything nibbly? Just a little something."

"Who are you asking?" Mom snickered. "Of course. There are chocolate chip cookies in the kitchen." I was already halfway out of the room by the time she finished.

"Good," I called out, getting a glass of milk. "I skipped dessert tonight."

"You?"

"Funny," I snorted. "Considering you're the one who got me hooked on the white stuff, woman."

"Wait. You skipped dessert..." Mom's face was stricken when I rejoined her. "Were you out tonight?"

"Yes? Is that okay?" I placed a plate of cookies on the coffee table.

"And you came here? What did Joe think?"

"It wasn't Joe, smarty. I wouldn't go to dinner with Joe."

"But breakfast is acceptable?"

"Sure. I mean, it's breakfast. Nobody goes on a romantic breakfast date."

"Any meal can be romantic if you put a little effort into it." There she was. Mom was back, and she'd be okay. I could breathe somewhat easier.

Even if the notion of a breakfast date with Joe filled me with confusion, making the bees buzz louder than ever. "It's not romantic for us. No, it was Deke I was out with."

"So he finally made it! And you chose to spend the evening with me? Instead of him?"

The accusation in her voice made me cringe a little. "Uh, you're welcome? Hey, I was worried about you. I wasn't in the mood for canoodling."

She rolled her eyes. "Honey. You have to take your life into consideration. I'm touched, really, that you came to see me. I can't tell you how much it means. But not at the expense of your life, for heaven's sake! I'd rather see you out having fun, developing your relationship with Deke. Not sitting around with Mom, who will be just fine."

"That's not my style." I shrugged with a grin.

She wasn't smiling. "I know. And it worries me."

"Why?"

"Because you need to work on your life. You have to have something for yourself, sweetheart. You can't live through the people you love. You also take too many chances for the people you care about. They don't even have to be close friends or relatives."

"Like who?"

She blinked rapidly. "Like Robbie Klein. Nate Patterson. Georgia Steel. Ring a bell? You get yourself mixed up in their lives and problems, at risk to your safety. Don't argue," she added, holding a hand up in front of my face. "You know as well as I that you were darn lucky to escape with nothing worse than a sprained wrist last time. You're a good person, honey, but your life is important. Your happiness is important. You can't attain happiness through other people."

"Funny. You're not the first person to give me that sort of speech tonight," I grumbled.

"Deke did? Good. You need to hear it from somebody who isn't your silly mother."

"Don't do that."

She gathered the ends of a throw blanket over her shoulders like she was donning armor. "Everybody thinks their mother is silly at times. I've accepted that. And I know I can go overboard—don't tell your sister I admitted it."

"My lips are sealed," I whispered, fighting a smile.

"Don't throw out the baby with the bathwater, is all I mean. My advice isn't nonsense. You have to build something for you, the way I did. You're already off to a great start. You turned your blog into something special, so special it caught the idea of a major publisher. Your articles are always well-received. You could become a famous food writer. I suspect you hold yourself back for my sake."

"What are you talking about?" Maybe I was a little huffy. Maybe a lot.

"You turn down work that would take you overseas, don't you? Or even across the country for more than a few days at a time."

Dang it. It was my turn to be evasive, the way she was earlier on. I studied the cookie in my hand like I'd never seen one before until the chips started melting against my skin.

"Do you deny it?" she murmured.

"How did this conversation take such a turn?" I asked. "Who squealed?"

"Raina."

"Raina? What the heck? She's gonna get an earful from me, no joke."

"She was concerned about you rejecting opportunities to expand your career, and I agree with her."

"Snitch," I muttered before taking a huge bite of cookie. Even the sweet, creamy chocolate and caramel notes from the brown sugar didn't do much to make me feel better. "Where does she get off calling you?"

"Don't talk with your mouth full, or you'll have my living room looking like a Jackson Pollock painting. His chocolate period." She handed me a napkin. "She was concerned, and hoping I could talk some sense into you."

"She's so lucky she isn't here right now."

"I agree," Mom repeated. "You have to expand your horizons. Don't be so worried about me, or the café. You're right. I should take on help. There are plenty of people who'd be glad for the chance to help. People who've retired but still want to be active. You should know. You see them all the time."

"True," I murmured. It was one of those moments when I didn't want to give too big a reaction, afraid she'd take it back. I didn't even want to move. "I'd love to see you ease up a little on yourself, too."

"And I would love to see you take life by the horns. Your life, finally." She put an arm around me and squeezed. "Don't be hard on Raina. She's only trying to be a good friend."

I held my tongue on that one.

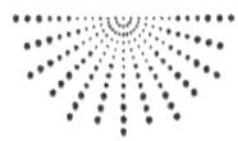

CHAPTER EIGHT

"I don't appreciate it."

"I was worried about you," Raina pouted. Not that I could see her pouting, per se, since we were only on the phone—instead of FaceTime—while I walked to the library.

"Then tell *me* about it. Not my mom."

"I did tell you! Remember? I very definitely expressed concern that you were closing yourself off from what could be fabulous opportunities. And you brushed me off."

"So you called my mom and tattled. Thanks a lot."

"Hey. I happen to love you and want the best for you. Though right now, I wonder why. And here I am, packing for a long weekend in Cape Hope. Maybe I should rethink my plans."

My resolve started to weaken. "That would be fun."

"Well, I did tell you I planned on coming down, didn't I?"

"You did."

"And I believe in keeping my word."

"You sure Nate won't mind?" I snickered.

"After what he's already put me through? He can wait a few days while I catch up with my bestie. Besides, I can always swing down and see him later. And he's neck-deep in the last phase of renovations. I'm so excited to see it."

"I can hardly wait myself." Having seen the "before" of the farmhouse and lands around it, it would be nice to replace those images with something fresh and new. Just as nice as it would be to see Nate realizing his hard-won dream.

"For now, I'm all about you, lady. And I can be down tonight, if that's okay."

"Of course it is! So long as you promise not to snitch on me ever again. We're not children."

"Says the girl who uses words like snitch." She laughed. "I can't promise, no matter how much you want me to. If I see you making a mistake I think you'll regret and there's no getting through to you, I'm gonna call on reinforcements. Just like I'd expect you to do the same."

"We'll never agree on this."

"Guess not," she agreed like it didn't mean anything. "I just want you to be happy. I can also help you juggle two men, if you need me."

"I'm not juggling two men."

"Says you," she snickered. "I'll book a room and let you know when I get in. Okay?"

"You're staying with me, obviously, and I don't want to hear another word. Why would you take the trouble of trying to find a room last-minute in the middle of tourist season?" Even though I was still more than slightly annoyed with her well-meaning ways, it would be fun to have her around.

And maybe. Just maybe. She'd be helpful when it came to juggling two guys, both of whom wanted my attention.

Deke and I weren't formally dating.

Joe and I weren't anything. He'd snickered when I called him a friend only days earlier.

Why did instinct tell me to keep them apart, then?

I strolled into the cool, quiet library, sighing with happiness at the scent of so many books. There was nothing like it. Technology was great—having an e-reader meant not having to pack a bunch of heavy books every time I went out of town—but nothing would ever replace the smell and feel of an actual book.

Nell noticed me right away. "What on earth is that?" she hissed, glancing around.

I looked down. "A stroller. With a dog inside. Do you not recognize Lola?"

"Emma." She looked at me from over the frames of her readers. "You can't be serious."

"You know how well-behaved she is. She won't bark. She won't do anything but sit there and be cute. Right, you little cotton head?" I bent down to give her a kiss, which she enthusiastically returned.

"You are entirely too much." Nell sighed.

"And hey, if it makes you feel better." I pointed out Lola's harness, which I'd attached to the stroller. "She can't jump out. We did the whole potty thing before leaving. She'll be good. I just hate leaving her alone, since we're apart whenever I leave town for work." My lower lip may or may not have jutted out in a world-class pout.

"Fine." She shrugged. "You wear me out."

I could've said the same thing about her, but chose not to. I knew better than to look a gift horse in the mouth. "Thank you. I'll be heading to the computers now to look up old periodicals."

"Help yourself." I caught her smiling as I wheeled the stroller away from the front desk.

"I told you it would be okay," I whispered to Lola. "And you were nervous about the looks we'd get." She looked up at me, completely uncomprehending.

And I did get a few looks, too, which told me it was time to stop talking to myself.

Several of the library's computers were in use when I got there, mostly young people who probably got kicked off the home computer and told to go out and do something with their time. So what did they do? They went to the library and settled back in.

One of the people using a terminal wasn't a kid. He wasn't a retiree, either, who normally comprised most of the library's patrons over the summer. I hung back for a second, smiling to myself at the sight of Joe Sullivan leaning in close, brows drawn together, staring intently at the screen in front of him.

"Excuse me, but you look like a detective who's supposed to be on vacation," I whispered as I wheeled the stroller over to him. "Also, you haven't been by to see our baby in ages."

His head snapped around, eyes wide. "Oh, no," he groaned, slumping a little as he took in the sight of me and the stroller. "You're sick."

"Funny, but I feel just fine." I parked the stroller next to him and sat on the other side. "What are you doing here?"

He made a big point of saying hi to Lola, who licked his hands until I was fairly sure he lost his fingerprints. "I had bacon with breakfast," he explained. "But I swear, I've washed my hands since then."

"Your hygiene is none of my business." I sniffed.

"Anyway, you got me thinking about that picture yesterday. Who it could've been. I've always been fascinated by the people who built summer homes down here. Can you imagine, taking an entire summer to stay in your house at the shore?"

"No. I can't imagine being able to do that," I admitted. "That entire time period fascinates me. I mean, let's not kid ourselves. There's lots of people nowadays who can do the same thing. It seems like there was so much more grace back then. Maybe we're looking at it through the lens of what we've been fed about that time."

"Maybe. Check it out." He pointed to his screen, where a photo of a badminton match being held on a sweeping lawn jumped out at me. "That's what they did. In long sleeves, long skirts, jackets. How did they manage it?"

"They didn't know any other way. Can you imagine a woman wearing a tee and shorts like I am now? She'd be branded a scarlet woman and ostracized."

"They're fairly short shorts, you know."

"Shut up. And no, they're not." I tugged them down

anyway, self-conscious. "I guess we weren't made for those times. Give me comfort any day. Oh, and a job and the right to vote and all that good stuff."

Somebody shushed us when he laughed, which of course made me laugh.

"Okay, you're a bad influence and I'm gonna get to work. I have some newspapers to look up." And I did, though I was aware of both him and the dog all the while. Every once in a while, she'd lick my arm, then lick his.

"What are you looking up?" he whispered, conscious of volume now that we'd been chastised.

"Obituaries."

"Fun."

I glanced over long enough to roll my eyes. "Mom thinks the girl in the picture looks like the last member of the family who owned that house. She passed away while I was in college. Evidently, it was the talk of the town. Everybody wanted to know who she left her fortune to, but there was never any indication."

"Oof. I can just imagine the storm that set off."

"Right? I'm sorta glad I wasn't here for it. All I know is, she didn't leave it to me or to anybody else in my family. I was hoping there'd be mention of it in the papers from back then."

He left me to my research, involved in his own. It wasn't hard to find all sorts of press about Millicent, since her family had practically founded the entire town generations earlier. The last handful of articles had to do with her death.

I made a mental note of her lawyer's name. Bernard Lewis. He wasn't local, but instead operated out of Philadelphia. A quick Google of his name told me he was still in his Center City office. The article named him as the will's executor.

The other two articles were pure speculation which had been written by—no surprise—Auntie Trixie. The first title made me rub the bridge of my nose, since it was enough to give me a headache. WHERE ARE MILLICENT'S MILLIONS?

Joe snickered, clearly reading what I'd pulled up on the screen. "Nice title," he whispered.

"Courtesy of Trixie Graham."

His eyes lit up in recognition of the lady he'd met a few times already, most recently in Paradise City. "Oh. Of course she did." A snort of laughter exploded from him even though he strained to cover it up. It was like a gunshot in the otherwise quiet library.

I turned my attention to the article, since I was afraid to make eye contact with anybody around us. It was bad enough I'd brought a dog in with me.

"Could you please control yourself? I have to live here. You don't."

"Sorry, sorry." But he was still working against the impulse to laugh, pressing his lips together, his cheeks puffing out.

There was nothing else in any of the articles that pointed to an answer regarding her fortune. It might as well have never existed. In Trixie's article she estimated Millicent's net worth at roughly twenty million dollars. A far cry from how wealthy the family used to be, but nothing to sneeze at.

"And it's all sitting somewhere," I whispered, more to myself than to Joe. "Unless the lawyer took it."

"You're always looking for a conspiracy," he whispered back.

"What's it sound like to you, detective? The woman was worth tens of millions—I know Trixie might've gone overboard with the headline, but she wouldn't throw a number out there without knowing for sure she was right. She's not irresponsible."

"And nobody knows what happened to her money," Joe murmured. He wasn't joking anymore. "No living relatives?"

"None."

"Then yeah, unless there's a record out there of the money being donated to charity, I'd go with the lawyer."

"Really?"

"I have no idea." He sighed. "Don't get yourself worked up. Maybe, I don't know, the money was supposed to go to somebody who was already dead, and they didn't have a will to dictate who it would go to. Maybe Millie didn't know they'd died—or maybe she did, and she just never got around to changing the document. Who knows?"

"Millicent," I whispered.

"Huh?"

"Somebody called her Millie once and got an iced tea thrown in their face. To her, it was a huge insult."

"She sounds charming. No wonder she didn't have a husband or kids."

"Shush."

Somebody cleared their throat in a very pointed way

from across the room. It was loud and obvious enough that I turned to see who'd done it.

I should've known. Nell fixed me with what I could only describe as a death glare.

I shrugged, grimacing, and mouthed, "Sorry!"

She shook her head before peering over the top of mine to see who sat on my other side.

A sly smile started to spread.

My eyes widened. Of course. She was thinking of seeing me with Deke last night, then Joe this morning. That little minx. I very deliberately dragged a finger across my throat, then pointed to her. She got the message and turned away. Smart thinking.

Though this didn't mean she wouldn't say something to Mom about it. And Trixie. And whoever else.

It was almost enough to make leaving the house less appealing.

"I'd better get going," I sighed, standing. "There's a little work I have to get done before Raina gets here later."

"Oh, she'll be in town? We should grab a slice on the boardwalk. Unless she's not a slice-on-the-boardwalk sort of person."

"She definitely is. Don't let the Birkin bag fool you. Oh, and keep tomorrow morning open."

He raised a brow. "Why?"

"I was thinking there's got to be a way to get you to relax more."

"I'm pretty relaxed right now…"

"I mean in everyday life. Real life. Not while you're on vacation."

His eyes narrowed. "Do I hate this idea? I think I might."

"You'll love it. Say goodbye to the grumpy detective, Lola." I lifted one of her front paws and waved it his way.

What would Raina think about Joe's invitation for pizza? I was sure she wouldn't leave me to wonder for long.

CHAPTER NINE

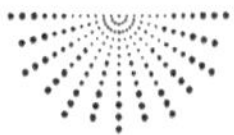

It was an absolute stunner of a day, which meant the sidewalks were peppered with tourists and towns-people alike as I pushed the stroller down the street. Sure, I could've taken the dog out, but then I'd have to contend with both a dog and a stroller.

Besides, she loved the attention. Less walking meant more time to observe, to sniff the air, to lick hands when offered. All she had to do was bask in her glory while I did all the work.

Not that it was work. She was all of twelve pounds.

Sure, I got my fair share of snickers, glances of disbelief. There might even have been pity in the faces of one or two people as I passed. Like they pitied the poor, childless girl who felt she had to push her dog in a stroller to make up for what she didn't have. People were like that. They tended to jump to conclusions.

For the most part, however, we were a hit. And I didn't

have to worry about her getting squished by window shoppers unaware of a ball of fur nearby.

A sense of pride tugged at my heart. This was my town, and these people thought highly enough of it to pay us a visit. It was the same every year, but different at the same time. Different people, different stories. At the heart, everybody just wanted to have a good time and escape the daily grind for a while.

In the middle of so many unfamiliar faces, one stuck out. I'd seen this face before—recently, in fact, as I absorbed the idea of her giving me a brother or sister.

She stood in front of a baby boutique on Main Street, looking into the window with a soft smile. It would be a shame to interrupt her when she was daydreaming about her life as a mother. The hope practically shining from her face told me everything I needed to know about how she felt about motherhood.

It was then that I knew without a shred of doubt that she'd be a good mother, and a good wife to Dad if they chose to get married. He was an old-school type of guy, and it would've surprised me to death if he didn't propose now that she was "in the family way," as they used to say.

Lola, ever the diplomat, chose that very second to let out the cutest little bark. Maybe it was because she was so small, but everything she did seemed cute to me.

Holly's head snapped around. When she noticed Lola, then me, the smile she'd worn before only widened. "Hi! Oh, my gosh, you're killing me with the cuteness!"

"So you don't think it's cheesy, me pushing her in a stroller?" I asked as I approached.

"Not at all. She'd get run over today, with all this foot traffic." Holly bent down to pet Lola's soft fur. "And who is this?"

"This is my baby, Lola."

Holly's face lit up. "She is precious! A Maltese?"

"Yeah! Not many people know that just from looking at her."

"I had a Maltese growing up. I'm allergic to dogs in general." She scratched Lola behind the ears, grinning. "What a sweetheart. Do you take her around with you a lot?"

"I had her at the library earlier, which went over… pretty much the way you'd expect bringing a dog to the library would go. But she's so well-behaved. She hangs out in the kitchen at the café when I work there."

Whoops. Had I said too much? A look came over her face, one that reminded me a lot of concern and guilt.

Time to change the subject. "How are you feeling?"

"Just great." She smiled again, relieved. "I was going to grab a little lunch before going back to work. Maybe a big lunch. My appetite is monstrous. It was like overnight, I went from not wanting to even think about food to wanting nothing but."

"I guess that's a good sign, huh?"

"That's what the doctor said."

Meanwhile, I couldn't help but notice a few glances our way. Unfriendly glances from people I recognized. Because who else but a Cape Hope resident would think there was anything even slightly wrong with two young women chatting with a dog between them?

Only the fact that my parents were so well-known—and the fact that I'd see these people again—kept me from telling them to mind their business. Was there something so wrong with talking to the woman? She was a good, sweet person who only wanted the same thing many women did. A home, a partner, a child, fulfilling work.

To live her life without the opinions of a bunch of strangers getting in the way.

I suppressed the urge to throw my arms around her, to protect her from them. She was a grown woman, but I couldn't help that protective instinct.

"Why don't we have lunch together? My treat. There's a table opening up across the street." I pointed to the restaurant in question, where diners enjoyed their salads and sandwiches while watching people walk past.

"You're sure?" She tucked a dark curl behind one ear, chewing her lip as she glanced over there. "I don't want to take up so much of your time."

"Don't even say that!" I scoffed. "Please. I offered, didn't I?" Yes, I had work to do, but this felt important. I told myself I'd have eaten at home just the same, and it would've taken time to make something. Knowing Holly had to go to work meant less chance of it turning into a length gab-fest, too.

"Okay, then." The poor thing looked dazed as we crossed the street. "This is so generous."

"Come on, you've made dinner for me how many times? If anything, I should be ashamed; I should've asked you two over ages ago to repay the favor. It seems like there's always something going on."

"Your dad is always talking about how interesting your work is. He's really proud, you know."

"Really?" We took a seat, with me parking the stroller beside me. "That's funny."

"Why is it funny?"

"Not funny ha-ha. Funny odd. He always wanted me to be a cop. I studied Criminal Justice to make him happy, even though I could never see myself solving cases and locking up the bad guys."

"And see, I think that's what's funny. Because you do solve cases. You've solved three so far."

"That's not the same."

"Isn't it? It sure sounds important where I'm sitting. You helped the people involved. He's proud of that too. But don't tell him I told you so," she giggled. "He'd accuse me of encouraging you."

"I won't say a word," I agreed. Dad? Proud of me? Here I was, thinking I was doing her a favor by inviting her to lunch, when she was the one making me feel better.

Holly ordered a chicken caesar salad, but only after making sure there was no raw egg in the dressing. "It comes out of a bottle." The server shrugged. I barely held back a laugh.

"I'll have the grilled chicken sandwich," I decided. "Fries. And a chocolate shake."

"Ooh, that sounds good," Holly mused. "Make that two shakes."

"I don't mean to be a bad influence!"

"You're not. I've been craving a shake forever—at least, that's how it feels. For once, I'll feel free to eat whatever I want. They'll have to roll me out of the house like a giant basketball by the time I'm full-term."

She was so thin, I had a hard time believing that. "Make sure Dad pampers you. I mean, the whole works. Rubbing your feet, rubbing your back, all of it."

"I don't think I'll need to make sure he does anything. He's already practically hanging on me. Don't get me wrong. I'm not complaining. I'm afraid he'll be the one needing a foot rub after all the running around he's bound to do. He already wants to start painting and decorating the nursery."

My heart ached just ever so slightly, though I made a point of smiling for her benefit. It was nice, really it was. It was also strange, thinking of him doing that for his child with a woman who wasn't my mom. "If anybody should know how to decorate, it would be you!"

"This is a little outside my area of expertise," she admitted. "I've been scouring the internet for ideas."

"That sounds like fun."

"You should come over and take a look once we get started," she offered. "I mean, if you're interested."

"I am!"

"Good! It would make him really happy, too." She had a good heart and wanted Dad to have his daughter with him through this. It wasn't so much about her being accepted as it was about him feeling comfortable, feeling like he had space and permission to love this new family.

How could I help but like somebody who loved him so much?

"I only wish I could get Darcy to come around," I admitted. "I know it must bother him—to put it mildly."

"Yes, that's pretty mild," she sighed. "He hopes she'll have a change of heart. So do I, of course—I want what he wants."

"Maybe she will. I think she will. She needs time to absorb this—it came as a surprise, though it probably shouldn't have. These things do happen, and you're not exactly over the hill." I leaned in, lowering my voice. "I hope this isn't too personal a question, but do you have a close relationship with your father?"

"Not at all. Don't think I don't know the psychology behind my falling in love with a man your father's age, either." She had a sense of humor about it, at least, or appeared to. I didn't know if I should laugh along with her or stay serious. I decided on a faint smile.

"I'm close with Dad, though Mom and I have always been closer. Darcy was Daddy's girl through and through. She adored him. He was her hero. Maybe because he was always busy with work—she clung to him when he was with us. She would've done anything to get his attention and keep it. When they divorced, it shocked her. I mean it really rocked her world, even though we were both grown up by then. She had this image in her head, you know?"

She nodded slowly. "Sure. I never knew my father, but of course I wanted him to be this rugged, handsome hero. Strong and solid and loving. Something happened to him, something kept him away from me. The things we tell ourselves when we're young." She tapped the side of her head. "It stays there."

"I guess that's why I've adjusted more quickly than she

has. I keep trying to get her to at least talk to him, but she shuts me down. I hope now she'll feel like there's more of a reason to do it."

"Or more of a reason to avoid him," Holly fretted.

"Leave it to me. You don't need anything to worry about now. Just think about my brother or sister, okay?"

Tears sparkled in her eyes. "Whichever they happen to be, they're already lucky to have you as their big sister."

"Okay, let's not both start crying!" I dabbed my eyes, then leaned in for a kiss from Lola. She sensed I was feeling emotional. When Holly reached over for a pet, she licked her palm.

"Be careful. I might kidnap this one," Holly grinned.

"Hey, if you'd be okay with it, I'd love to leave her with you guys while I'm on one of my trips. I usually leave her with Mom or Darcy, but it's not like I have a contract with them or anything." Did I shoot myself in the foot by saying it? Probably. Would Mom act like I'd delivered a personal affront if and when she found out Lola—her grandpuppy—was with the enemy? Probably.

Did I have a bad habit of going out of my way to make other people happy? More than probably.

The food came then, which Holly dug into with a level of intensity I'd never seen from her. The baby had definitely affected her appetite. "You want some fries? There's so many, they're practically falling off the plate."

"Maybe just a couple." She proceeded to dip a fry into her milkshake like it was ketchup. My kind of girl.

"Hey. Do you think it would be okay for me to visit the Montbatten house while you're there sometime? I won't touch anything. I promise. I'm sort of obsessed with it right now."

"The picture you were talking about?"

"Yeah. Besides, I've always wanted to go in there. It's gotta be stunning inside."

"Oh, it is. Breathtaking. Sure, you can come by any time you want. Just let me know." She dunked another fry. "I wish they hadn't cleared the house of Millicent's possessions after she died. It would've been nice to have a room dedicated to her, the last Montbatten. How she lived, what she liked. She was a huge reader, from what I understand, and her book collection was extensive. Now, it's gone."

"Really?" There went that hive of bees in my head, kicked over again by the most innocent comment. "Ooh, I wonder if the book that picture was in belonged to her! It would make perfect sense. Mom said the girl in it resembled her. I didn't find any pictures of her in the papers I looked through at the library."

"There you go, jumping in feet first." She shook her head with a smile. "By now, I wouldn't expect anything less."

CHAPTER TEN

"It must be cool, working around books all day," Raina mused as we walked down Main Street.

"Darcy would probably say the same about your line of work—heck, so would I," I added with a snort.

"Don't get me wrong. I love what I do, and I'm lucky. Still, I'd love the chance to be surrounded by books every day." She made grabby hands. "Maybe I should've brought a tote with me to carry some home."

"Darce will be more than happy to sell you one with the First Edition logo printed on it," I pointed out with a smirk. "Go nuts."

"I just might. Remind me why we absolutely have to stop by right this very minute, though? Not that I mind," she added. "But it would've been nice to take a minute and sit down before you dragged me from the apartment."

"I'd hardly say I dragged you. We're going to see if there are any more books like the one I found the other day. I don't think anybody's come to take them away yet. I remember seeing more than a few old ones scattered around."

"You think the books belonged to this Millicent person?"

"I have a hunch. Holly said her possessions were cleared out when she died. Darcy had just opened the shop around that time. Some of the used books have been sitting there for years. Millicent's could be among them. I'm almost completely sure the one I found was hers. Why else would there be a picture of her in there?"

"You still don't know it was her. You only think it was."

"Hmm." I eyed her warily as we crossed the street, arriving at the block where the café and bookstore sat side-by-side. "Maybe I should've left you at the apartment, after all."

"Hush." She tossed her impressive mane of chocolate hair over one shoulder. "You know I'm always down for a mystery. I don't want to see you get your hopes up, is all. This might turn out to be nothing."

"Or it might turn out to be something huge!"

"I love you." She slung an arm around my waist. "I really do. And I've missed you. Rome is nice, but hanging out with you is like therapy."

"I don't know if that feels like a compliment or what."

"I meant it as one. You center me. And my energy's always peppier when we're together."

"Good. I'll need you to be peppy and energetic when we eat pizza with Detective Joe on the boardwalk."

"What?" she asked as I opened the door to the store.

"We'll talk about it later," I whispered, ignoring her pointed stare in favor of looking for Darcy. She, like Mom, would've done herself a favor by hiring more help. One of the two high school girls she'd brought on for the summer had register duty, while Darcy helped one of several customers clamoring for her attention.

"It's so good to see her," Raina murmured. And it was, even if my sister looked completely frazzled. I knew she thrived on it, the way Mom did. We hung back, perusing a few books, until the rush calmed a little.

And she turned to us.

And the temperature dropped a good twenty degrees.

Raina didn't notice, probably because the chill wasn't directed at her. "Hi!" She gave Darcy a hug. "It's good to see you! This place is jumping!"

"It's been like this the last few days," Darcy grinned. "It's exhausting, but I'd be crazy to complain."

"Uh, hi?" I muttered, waving a hand since my sister had yet to acknowledge me.

"Hey." She turned her attention back to Raina. "I didn't know you were coming to town."

"It was sort of a sudden decision," Raina explained. She was starting to get a feel for what was going on, clearly, and she sounded uncomfortable. I couldn't blame her.

"Well, it's not like Emma would've told me even if you'd made plans in advance. She tends not to tell me things."

"Okay." Raina looked from her to me and back again. "Uh, can you direct me to the used books which haven't been donated yet? We were hoping to find some old books like the one Emma found. The one with the photo in it."

"Oh, sure." Darcy pointed toward the back corner of the shop, where the boxes still waited behind a makeshift barricade so nobody would get hurt. "I remember seeing a bunch of those old books, with the old bindings and covers. But they're all mixed up in different boxes."

"It's okay. I have plenty of time." She wasted no time hurrying away, obviously wanting to get away from us.

"I'm really busy, as you can see." It would've been nice to believe my sister didn't mean to bump into me as she passed, but I wasn't naïve.

"We obviously need to talk," I whispered, following her.

"Now isn't the time."

"No. You'd rather be childish."

She whirled on me, which was awkward since I was much closer than she expected. We bumped into each other. "I'm at work, Emma. I know you have a hard time understanding that the entire world doesn't stop turning for you."

"Where is this coming from? What, is it because I wanted to wait to tell you about the baby? I'm sorry you found out the way you did."

"And you just had to have lunch with her today, didn't you? Right out there on the sidewalk, where everybody could see." Her eyes narrowed. "Why would you do that?"

I almost laughed, it struck me as so ridiculous. "Darce! You sound like I was dancing naked for all the world to see! Holy jeez."

"You're spitting in Mom's face by doing that," she hissed.

"I'm not. I'm trying to be nice. To Dad's girlfriend. To the mother of our baby sibling."

"Half-sibling." Her jaw was set hard enough to crack a walnut.

I was speechless. Sure, she was never unclear on her

feelings about Dad and the divorce. But this? I was glad when a customer approached with a question for her to answer. In the blink of an eye, she went back to her normal, helpful, cheerful self.

But that didn't last long. She turned to me again, and her eyes were spitting fire. "We already know which side you fall on. You don't need to flaunt it in front of everybody."

It took a real struggle to contain myself. Years of trying to gently talk her into being mature came flooding back at once. Years of being patient, trying to encourage her, being aware of her feelings smacked crashed into me like a wave.

I took her by the arm and pulled her away from the busier section we stood in, then practically shoved her into the corner. Enough was enough. "Darcy, I love you very much. But you need to grow up. You talk about me thinking the world stops when I want it to, but look at you. You expect me to be cold and ignorant toward a really nice, sweet person who just wants to be happy. And she makes Dad happy—very happy. He loves her. That doesn't mean he doesn't love you anymore."

Her breath caught. "Don't even—"

"I'm still talking," I hissed. "I'm sick to death of tiptoeing around you on this. I won't ignore her. I won't be mean. I'll support her, because we both love Dad. That gives us something in common. And if you'd grow up for a minute and remember the divorce had nothing to do with you, you'd figure out everything you're missing out on by closing them out of your life."

"It had nothing to do with me?" she whispered, eyes wide like she couldn't believe it.

"Yeah. You were in your twenties, for God's sake. We're not the result of a broken home. They did their best, both of them, for our sake. This isn't about you. Stop acting like you only care about Mom, because we both know that's not true."

Her face fell. "You need to get out of here. Now."

"Gladly." I spun on my heel and marched out, tears of rage blurring my vision. Raina saw me—I caught her out of the corner of my eye, her eyes wide and her mouth falling open.

Rather than wait for her, I walked outside and doubled back around the building through the alley, which led me to the back door of the café. It was unlocked, the way Mom usually left it during the day in case deliveries came through.

She must've heard me slam the door closed, since she joined me roughly three seconds later, just as I was flopping down on a stool and resting my head on my arms against the prep table. The metal was blessedly cool compared to the flush on my cheeks.

"Honey! What's the matter?" Mom was by my side in a second, arms around me. "What happened?"

"I'm so mad at her!" I gasped. "I've never been so mad at her!"

"Your sister?" She clicked her tongue. "Yes, she came over to tell me about your lunch with Holly."

"Don't tell me you're mad, too," I begged, my head still down.

"Not at all. It's just the sort of thing you would do." She hugged me, sighing. "I don't blame that girl. I don't. I can't see us ever being friends, exactly, but I can at least appreciate you making the effort to be friends. You're braver than I ever was."

"Braver?" I lifted my head, and she ran her hands over my cheeks to loosen the strands of hair that were stuck on them thanks to my tears. It reminded me of being little again, sweaty and suddenly heartsick, needing Mom's calm and love.

"Sure! Sitting out there with her, for everyone to see. Sending a message. I'm so proud of you." She kissed my forehead. "No matter how many times I remind people that I don't hold anything against Holly, they can't stop supposedly freezing her out on my account. I thought things were getting better. But now..."

"It's like the early days all over again. I know."

"Wash your face, cool yourself down." Another kiss, then she hurried back out to the counter.

I did as she ordered, and the cold water I used to splash my cheeks did wonders. Nobody could upset me worse than Darcy, probably because we normally got along so well.

Minutes later, I was weighing dry ingredients for the goods that would be baked for the following day—baking, even prep work, always calmed me—when Raina walked in from the dining room. "Wow. I think I'm glad I wasn't there for what happened. I hope you're not mad over my ducking away."

"Not at all." I set aside the muffin ingredients after whisking them together. "It wasn't your fight. You don't need to get in the middle of my family stuff."

"Well, I don't have a sister so I have no idea what you're going through. But!" She wiggled her fingers around in my face. "I come bearing gifts. A gift. One gift."

I had to laugh. "What did you find?"

She reached into her shoulder bag and pulled out a book. Like the one I'd found, it was without a dust jacket and its cover was well-worn. "Is this the sort of thing you were looking for?"

"Sure!" I flipped it open. *Wuthering Heights.* "I wonder if this was hers. The cover's all rubbed clean, just like *The Scarlett Letter.*" I shook the pages, disappointed when nothing came out. "Oh."

"What's wrong?"

"I was hoping there was something inside. Another picture. Something."

"Oh, there totally was." Her smile was wicked, knowing, as she reached back into her bag.

"You jerk!"

"Hey. I don't like to reveal everything at once."

"That makes me feel sorry for Nate."

She scowled. "There are knives nearby. Watch it. I might not even give you this letter that I found tucked inside the book."

My eyes almost fell out. "A letter?"

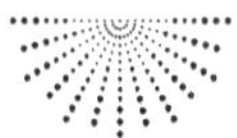

*F*rank,

By now, you know of my condition. You can't imagine the disappointment I suffered—and still suffer—now that I know for certain how you feel about the matter.

About myself, as well.

Could you have played me false all along? Were your loving words nothing but a sweet lie? I know well of the lies men tell women when it comes to such situations as ours. I never thought I'd be one of them.

Is that what hurts worst of all? Knowing what a fool I was? How I believed you. How I trusted you. I opened myself to you in every possible way, and you used me for your pleasure. You said all the right things. The look in your eye spoke of love.

What an actor you are. You might make your living on the stage or in the movies. Your mantel would collapse under the weight of so many awards. How could you do this to me? Did those days in the garden mean nothing? Can you honestly say it was all a charade on your part?

You've left me with nothing. With no one. The child will be surrendered for adoption upon birth—Father has arranged for that. To think! I feared he would kill you when he sought you out. I demanded to join him. How I wept, pleaded, swearing over the truth of our love.

He was right all along. You were a cad. You thought you might use me, perhaps gain a bit of my fortune, and run away. Now, you'll receive nothing. Not even the sight of your child. Our child.

I would say I hate you but you are beneath hatred. Beneath loathing. You do not deserve my hatred.

"There's no signature," I whispered. "It ends there."

"Holy smokes." Raina drew her feet up under her, a glass of wine in one hand. We were both in our pajamas with a pizza from the shop downstairs on the coffee table. Lola danced around, hoping to get lucky with a dropped bit of pepperoni or cheese.

Like I wanted to deal with the issues that would stir up.

"I mean, the paper's practically burning up in my hand." I snickered, turning it around to look at the blank back side. "The poor girl."

"No signature?"

"None." And the envelope was blank, too. Fragile, yellowed with age. "She wrote it, but never sent it or even finished the thing."

"Maybe this was a draft. Nothing more. She might've written another one and sent it off." Raina huffed. "I hope she did. I hope she did worse than that. Frank. I never did like that name."

I was careful to put the letter back in its envelope, then

tucked it into the book where it had sat since who knew when. Maybe since the day she wrote it. Poor girl.

Once the letter was safe, I sat down to eat another slice. "Did you see how happy Mr. Angelo was to see me?" I laughed. "Goes to show you how often I was down there in the weeks after the breakup. I might as well have set up an air mattress on the floor."

"I can understand why you would. This is good stuff." She paused before biting into her second slice. "Oh, hold up. Didn't you say Joe wanted to have pizza on the boardwalk?"

"So?" I asked, chewing. "What, you can't eat pizza twice in one weekend? After gorging yourself in Rome?"

She thought about it for maybe two seconds before taking a bite. "Yeah, that's the problem. I need to work off the extra calories."

"Don't worry. I'll keep you busy. You can come to the yoga studio with me tomorrow."

"Yoga?" She held a napkin over her mouth in case anything shot out while she laughed hysterically.

"Thanks," I muttered, rolling my eyes.

"I'm surprised, is all. You, willingly doing yoga."

"It's for Joe's sake. He needs to find ways to relax and center himself when he's working. No more panic attacks." I glanced her way and found her staring at me with a smirk. "What?"

"You care an awful lot."

"Why not? Even I can admit he's saved my bacon. Why not do what I can? Besides, tell me the thought of him doing yoga isn't hilarious."

"Even funnier than the thought of you doing it," she

snorted.

"Careful. You might choke while laughing at me. What a tragedy that would be."

"All right, fine." She got serious. "I think it's nice that you care. Hopefully he'll take to it. But yoga's never been my thing. You know that."

"You're into meditating!"

"Which is not the same. I've never cared for it." She tipped her head to the side. "But I'd be happy to show him how to do that, come to think of it."

"That's a good idea. He needs all the help he can get, working in a high-pressure town like that. When I think of how worried I used to get over Dad going to work…" I shook my head.

My gaze fell on the envelope, sitting on the dining room table. I didn't have a dining room—except for the bedroom and bathroom, the apartment was an open floor plan—so I could see it from where we sat.

"I wonder if it was Millicent. I wish whoever had cleared out the house hadn't been so dumb about it. I wonder if there's a sample of her handwriting somewhere."

"Where would you find something like that?"

"No idea. If her things were still kept somewhere, I might land on something and compare it to this letter."

Raina grew silent, carefully pulling a piece of pepperoni away from gooey, stretchy cheese. "I feel so bad for her."

"Me, too. That poor thing. He told her he loved her. It sounds like her dad went to have it out with him—maybe to tell him he had to marry her or something. And Frank backed out. I wonder how he managed it."

"Who knows? Maybe his family was rich, too, and they didn't want him marrying her. She was loose or whatever they called it."

"But she was rich. It would've been a good match as far as that went. And unless he was a billionaire, she was probably better off than him."

"Maybe he was already engaged to somebody else."

"Could be," I agreed. "Either way, it's a sad situation. The baby was put up for adoption, supposedly."

We turned to each other at the same time. I didn't know how I looked, of course, but I suspected I was as wide-eyed and surprised looking as she was. "What if we could find the baby? What if they're owed money or something?"

Her eyes lit up—then immediately dimmed. "How would we ever do that? We don't even know if she had a boy or a girl. We don't even know if it was Millicent or not! I think we're getting ahead of ourselves."

I hated how right she was. "Okay. Hang on." I got up and went to the junk drawer, where I knew there was a notepad waiting. "Let's make a list."

"Would you please give that poor dog something before she spins herself sick? Or slams her poor little head into something?" Sure enough, Lola was spinning in mad circles, half-crazy over the scent of pizza she couldn't enjoy.

"I'm sorry, baby." I crouched in front of her. "No pizza for you. Your little tummy can't handle it. I don't want you to get sick."

I looked up at Raina. "And I don't feel like cleaning it up."

A minute later, Lola had her dinner and I was back on the couch with my notepad. "Okay," I said as I clicked the pen. "Where do we start? We have to find out for sure whether it was Millicent in the picture."

"Right." Raina watched as I wrote this down.

"Once we find that out," I murmured, tapping the pen against my chin. "We have to find out where she had the baby."

"And when," Raina added.

This was starting to look overwhelming. "Did she have a boy or a girl?" I asked as I continued to write.

"And what happened to them?"

"Holy jeez. We're never gonna be able to do this. We're talking about records from, what? Sixty years ago? Seventy?" I tossed the notepad onto the coffee table, disappointed. "It's impossible."

"That doesn't sound like you." She leaned over and picked up the pad. "I think there's something else that needs to be done after we confirm this was Millicent, and before any records are looked into."

"What else is there?" I asked, rubbing my temples.

"What were the terms of her will? Did she leave her money to the baby? This is what I meant when I said we're getting ahead of ourselves."

At least she used the word *we*. She didn't make me feel like a nerd for letting my imagination run away with me. "You're right. Looks like I'm going in to Philly soon to visit that lawyer of hers."

"Has anybody ever told you you're like a dog digging for a bone once you get an idea in your head?"

"You're the first one today," I shrugged.

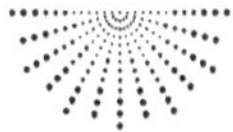

CHAPTER TWELVE

The look on Joe's face when I approached him, standing in front of Breanna Schultz's yoga studio, was maybe one of the top three funniest things I'd ever seen. I had to stop and bend at the waist, laughing until my sides hurt.

"Oh? This is funny to you?" He looked at the building, then at me. "You want me to do yoga?"

"Listen. It's good for relaxation and connecting to your breathing."

"And what does that have to do with me? Why do I wanna connect to my breathing?" He rolled his eyes like this was all so utterly beneath him.

"So you'll be able to calm yourself down when you need to. When you're feeling overwhelmed, you'll more easily connect to your center. To yourself. Not the part of you getting all caught up in the madness around you." I grasped the door handle. "This is all for your sake. I don't like yoga at all."

"Then why the hell are you asking me to do it?"

"For the same reason people eat greens when they don't feel like it. Because it's good for them." I opened the door. "Stop complaining and come on."

"You're maybe the worst person."

"I've been called worse than that lately." At least he didn't ask what I meant; he was probably too busy having his second panic attack at the thought of, God forbid, bending for a little while.

Darcy's comments still stung. A lot. We'd fought before, the way all siblings did, but she'd never been vicious like that. Personal.

"Hey." I stopped him before we entered the room where Breanna taught her beginners class three days a week. "Do you think I think the world revolves around me? Like I'm self-centered?"

"You're really asking me this while you're about to force me into something I really, deeply don't want to do?" He was grinning until he saw I wasn't kidding. In a flash, he turned into Detective Joe, right down to the stern expression. "No. Absolutely not. You're the least selfish person I've ever met."

That was nice to hear, though I had a feeling he was exaggerating. But it made me feel better.

"Emma!" Breanna was all smiles when she found us standing outside the room where she was prepping the music. "You're here! I'm so glad."

Then, she laid eyes on Joe. The man was like walking, talking magic. She went from smiley and friendly to a deep-voiced vamp. "Hi. I think I've seen you around. You're

Emma's friend, the detective." If she'd batted her eyelashes or pulled out a cigarette on one of those long holders and asked for a light, I wouldn't have been surprised.

"You can call me Joe," he grinned. How did he manage to be so cool in the face of obvious female lust?

I cleared my throat, feeling like a third wheel all of a sudden. "Joe's new to this whole thing."

"You're practically new, yourself," she teased before laughing way, way harder than her joke warranted. I'd never had a problem laughing at myself when the situation called for it. Sometimes I was the first person to do the laughing. But this?

I plastered on a wide smile and ignored Joe's knowing smirk. "Then I guess we're in the right place, huh?" I asked, marching into the room where a handful of women were chatting.

Chatter which stopped dead the second Joe walked into their midst. I had the feeling he'd become a fan of yoga by the time the class was over. Leave it to me to lead him to it.

"Here." I thrust a mat his way.

"Do you just happen to have two yoga mats at your place?" he whispered, unrolling it the way I unrolled mine.

"Yes."

"Why?"

"Because I liked this color better," I explained, unrolling my light pink mat while he had the purple.

"A wise decision, especially considering you never use them."

"You don't know my life." I did what I could to get to the yoga state of mind while also doing what I could to ignore his snickers, and the appraising looks still coming from the other side of the room. It was clear the women who'd already set up their mats wished there was a way they could move closer to him without looking obvious. A few of them shimmied, but that was the thing about an anti-slip mat. It stayed in place.

"Good morning!" Breanna's voice was warm, confident. "We have a first-timer here with us this morning, so I'll make it a point to take a little more time with him."

Oh, boy. How did I not see this happening? I glanced at Joe, who looked like he was barely fighting back a grin. Well, of course he would like that. Breanna was tall, willowy, with the body of somebody who made yoga her lifestyle.

Me? Muffins were my lifestyle. In the back of my mind, my mother's voice rang out, reminding me that my youthful metabolism would eventually betray me. I would hit thirty and suddenly, everything I ate would show itself on my hips, thighs, tummy.

First, we practiced some deep breathing to center ourselves. Soft chanting emanated from Breanna's phone, positioned at the front of the room. I tried to get myself into the proper headspace, to ignore Joe and the other people in the room in favor of going deeper into my own mind.

It was a real mess in there. Sort of like when a person cleaned their apartment and shoved everything in the closet to hide it. My mind was that closet. I was afraid to open the door, in case everything came falling out at once like in a cartoon.

"Now, we'll start with sun salutations." Breanna stood

between Joe and me, walking him through the progression of poses. "Really stretch while keeping your heels on the floor. I'm going to put my hands on your hips and pull them back—just try to relax."

Meanwhile, I was also in downward dog. I turned my head slightly to look over at Joe, whose face was a mask of confusion and frustration. A giggle bubbled up in my chest, though I managed to turn my face away before he saw me fighting a laugh.

"Okay, now you're going to down between your arms, dropping your hips, leaving everything from your pelvis down flat on the floor." Breanna positioned herself in front of Joe, showing him how to move into cobra pose. She arched her back and threw back her head, basically thrusting her chest toward him.

What made it hilarious was the way he cleared his throat, his face going red.

We went through this again and again until he actually seemed to have the moves down, if not the flow between them. "Relax, focus on your breathing, ease into it. This should not be stressful. There is no strain."

Easy for her to say. I was sweating after fifteen minutes.

Another fifteen minutes later, we were finished. Thank God for that, since I was a mess. We ended the class in child's pose, which allowed me to compose myself a little bit and get my breathing under control. I really needed to start taking better care of myself—after all, Lola depended on me. I had somebody to take care of.

"Great class, everybody!" Breanna clapped softly, and the

others joined in. Joe didn't, I noticed, but at least he wasn't flushed and sweaty the way I was.

"Isn't this supposed to be relaxing?" he whispered. "You look like you just went ten rounds with a heavyweight. And I know I'm going to feel this tomorrow. Maybe later today, even."

"It gets easier the more you do it," I reasoned.

"Though you aren't speaking from experience."

I stuck my tongue out at him as I rolled my mat up. "Anyway, that's your first yoga practice. What do you think?"

"Honestly? I can see how the whole experience would be helpful. The soft music, stretching—"

"A woman's hands on your hips, pulling them back until your butt is flush against her nether regions."

"Quiet," he warned as Breanna approached. She was positively radiant, glowing, exuding good health and vitality. Why did I want to smack her?

"You did terrific for your first time," she praised with a wide smile. "Will we be seeing you again?"

"I'm only in town on vacation," he admitted. "Normally, I'm up the road in Paradise City."

"Oh, of course." Her face fell a little. "Well, you're always welcome here. You seem to really have an affinity for the practice. Eventually, you'll be able to do an entire hour-long class."

I had to turn away when Joe's face went slack. "An entire hour?"

"Maybe we should get going," I suggested. "I promised

Mom I would stop by to make sure she didn't need any help."

"Great, I could go for a muffin. I think I earned it after all that hard work."

From the way Breanna giggled, I guessed he winked or did something similarly sexy. Not that I cared.

We started walking down the street, and at first we didn't say much to each other. Companionable silence was nice, the feeling that one didn't need to always be talking.

Naturally, he broke it moments after I had that thought.

"Do you not like her very much?"

"Who?"

"Breanna. Why did you take me to her studio if you don't like her?"

"I like her just fine. I'm sure if my head wasn't always in a hundred different places, we could be friends. I need to make more of an effort in that direction." I looked over at him. "What made you say I don't like her?"

"You seemed sort of short-tempered. Annoyed."

"Well, I'm sorry, but she couldn't have been more obvious. Listen, it's none of my business and I know it. But I've never been able to stomach the sight or sound of a woman making a fool out of herself."

"How did she do that?"

For a second, I thought for sure he was only teasing, only trying to get my goat. There wasn't a hint of a smile on his face. "Are you serious?"

That was when he snickered. "You sound jealous."

"What would I have to be jealous of? A woman blatantly

throwing herself at you? Yeah, wow, that's something to be jealous of."

He was still chuckling, and still making me want to push him out into traffic, when we walked into the café. I was glad our route didn't take us past the bookstore, since I didn't even want to see my sister through the window.

"Detective Joe! It's so good to see you!" Mom practically burst at the seams at the site of Joe. Though not before giving me a look of approval which I hoped he didn't pick up on.

"Mrs. Harmon, your daughter has been running me ragged this morning. Can you believe she actually made me do yoga?" He groaned, leaning against the counter like a man who had just run his first marathon.

"Now, now." She shook her finger, chiding him if only jokingly. "It's good for you. You need to learn to relax. Your health is very important."

"You're absolutely right. However, right now all I want in the world is one of your blueberry muffins. And since my health is so important, I'll stop at only one even though I want two." With a smile like his, there was no denying him anything. My mother was always a sucker for a good smile.

For that matter, so was I.

I left them to their banter in favor of looking around the café. It was Friday morning, which was always a strange time. The people who'd come in for a week's vacation on Saturday were normally wrapping it up by now, while those who liked to take Fridays off in the summer to get down to the shore that much earlier were already starting to trickle into town. The customers seated at the dozen scattered tables were a mixture of townsfolk and tourists.

One of those townsfolk wasn't to be missed anywhere. Her hats always made her stick out like a sore thumb.

"Mrs. Merriweather, good morning." I sat across from her. "I'm not going to take up too much of your time."

"You can take all of my time! I always enjoy chatting with you." She leaned in, looking Joe's way. "Congratulations. He is quite a catch."

Dear Lord, I prayed he couldn't hear her. He seemed invested in whatever he was talking about with Mom, thank goodness. "Now, Mrs. Merriweather. It's not like you to spread gossip." That was a bald-faced lie. "He's not a catch. I haven't caught him. And I'm not trying to, either, so don't get any ideas."

She sighed. "Youth is wasted on the young. If only we could trade places. I would show you how it's done."

I had no doubt. "Anyway," I chuckled, "I was wondering something. Were you well acquainted with Millicent Montbatten?"

Her face lit up, though in a different way than it did when she was talking about past conquests. "Certainly! We were girls together. Oh, she was lovely. Nothing like that stodgy father of hers. Always telling her what to do, while her mother never had any backbone." She shook her head, clicking her tongue. "Were it not for him, she might have married one day."

"Why do you think it had anything to do with him?" I asked, barely able to contain myself. Here was somebody who was actually there back in those days, somebody who held a wealth of information.

"No one was a good enough for him. He even sent her away for a while, to Philadelphia, where she could stay with his sister and meet suitable young men. Oh, Millie was furious. She never cared for her aunt, or for that social circle. By the time he passed away and she was free to do as she wished, I suppose she was too set in her ways. She couldn't see her way to learning to compromise with someone else. I was busy with my family and my children at the time, and I do regret our growing apart."

"That's a shame," I murmured. Poor Millie. "Was there ever a man named Frank in her life?"

She frowned, her face practically collapsing into wrinkles. "Frank? The only Frank I remember was the gardener's son. There was no Francis, Franklin. Not that I can recall."

If there was one person whose memory I trusted, it was hers. The woman was sharp as a tack, even at her age. "And you say her father sent her to Philadelphia? How long was she gone, can you remember?"

"Certainly, since that was the summer I was married. I did so want her to be there, but there was no denying that man when he set his mind to something. She left in late winter, and didn't return until autumn."

A theory was starting to build in my head. "Thank you so much, I love talking about those times."

"Well, feel free to pick my brain anytime you want. It's nice for an old lady to feel like her memories won't go with her." She stood then, shaking invisible wrinkles from her flowy, flower printed caftan. "As much as I hate to leave now, with so much delicious eye candy on display, I have some visiting to do."

Eye candy. The woman was a trip.

At the last second, something occurred to me. "Do you remember Frank's last name?"

"Welburn. His father was Mr. Welburn." She patted my hand. "Remember: don't waste your youth. Grab him while you have a chance." Her faded blue eyes sparkled, making me wonder what it would have been like to know her when she was young. I had the feeling we would've been friends.

I followed her out the door with my eyes, and watched as someone who was just on his way into the café held the door for her. She expressed her gratitude, touching his arm and calling him a gentleman.

Sure, he was a gentleman.

He also happened to be Deke Bellingham.

And when he found Joe approaching the table to sit where Mrs. Merriweather had just been sitting, his smile turned to a frown.

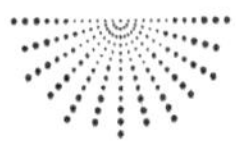

CHAPTER THIRTEEN

U h-oh.

"Hey!" I called out, waving. "Good morning."

He seemed hardly impressed, focusing on Joe who by now had noticed him, too. "Yeah, good morning. I thought I might find you here today."

I let out a nervous chuckle, glancing over at my mom who of course was watching this play out. Would she help me somehow? Of course not. She was too busy observing. "I worked here during the early rush."

"Then she introduced me to yoga, which I'm not sure if I should thank her for or what." Joe stood, extending hand for Deke to shake. "Good to see you again, Deke."

"Yeah, same here." Not only did his insincerity practically ring out for everybody to hear, but he was still frowning as he shook Joe's hand.

"Here, sit down. You want something to drink? I could get it for you." Heck, I would've gladly run all the way down to the boardwalk and gotten him a funnel cake. Or maybe flown to Paris for croissants. Anything to get away from that table, where two men stared each other down while trying to make it look like they weren't.

"Emma? Can you help me here?" There were a handful of people waiting at the counter, looking like they were all part of the same group. Probably a family on their way home that morning, hoping to beat the traffic.

"Gladly," I called out, hurrying to the kitchen to wash my hands before filling orders.

"What in heaven's name is that about?" she hissed as we passed each other behind the counter.

"You're asking me?"

"Has Deke committed to anything?"

"No! You don't think I would've said something if that was the case?"

"How would I know? You're awfully selective about what you will and won't share."

"Now's not the time to get offended," I muttered, watching them out of the corner of my eye. They just… sat there. Joe asked a question, Deke answered. Deke said something, Joe nodded in agreement. The iciness was enough to make me shiver.

"Maybe they're both terrible when it comes to small talk?" she suggested, which got nothing but an eye roll out of me.

The fact was, while I didn't really technically owe either of them anything, Deke's presence while Joe happened to be in the café at the same time had made my stomach clench, hadn't it? Which meant I knew there was something wrong about this whole situation even if I didn't want to admit to myself.

But I was only friends with Joe. Wasn't I?

And Deke and I were only casually seeing each other. And only when our schedules permitted. That was the way it had always been.

So why did I feel like I had been unfaithful to both of them?

Once we had the family taken care of, I poured a coffee and brought it to the table. "Black, just the way you like it."

Deke turned his full attention on me, smiling. But it was a tight smile, insincere. "Thanks. I was just on my way around town, admiring the scenery. I think I'll take this to go."

"You don't have to." But he was already standing, waving to Mom and thanking her for the coffee while on his way across the room. I shot Joe a pleading look before hurrying out the door after Deke.

"Deke, you don't have to leave. I wish you wouldn't."

He stopped, his back to me. "What's going on there?" he asked.

"Nothing. He's a friend. He's in town this week."

That was enough to make him turn around and glare at me. Those pretty, gold flecks in his eyes weren't so pretty when he looked mad enough to spit fire. "Don't you think you could've told me about that? That there was another guy in town, wanting your time and attention?"

Well. I could be apologetic when the situation called for it, but this is not that situation. I felt my chin jutting out, while my hands found my hips. "Hold on just a second. For one thing, I didn't know he was coming in. That was a surprise. For another thing, you are so vague about if and when you would decide to grace me with your presence. I didn't even know for sure until you strolled into the café whether or not you actually planned on visiting for sure. Who knew? Maybe something would come up and you'd suddenly leave the country and I wouldn't know. Or maybe Marsha would send you off on assignment and you'd drop everything and go. Either way, I don't owe you an explanation. If you wanted all my time this week, you should've told me. And even if you had told me, I would've told you that I still have a life here. I can't drop everything."

He backed away, shaking his head. "Well, don't let me take up any more of your time this morning."

"I won't." I spun on my heel, determined to march into the café and plop down in front of Joe. Only Joe was on his way out the door.

"Where are you going?" I asked. "You didn't even finish your muffin."

"Yeah, my eyes were bigger than my stomach. I'll see you later." He barely even looked at me before starting down the sidewalk.

"Wait!" I trotted beside him. "Don't do this. I know you're mad about something. Do you have a problem with Deke? I didn't know anything about that."

"I don't have a problem with him. Okay?"

"Then what's the matter? Why won't you talk to me?"

He stopped, turning to face me, and I suddenly wished I hadn't followed him. He had his Detective Joe face on. "How come you told me there wasn't anything happening with you two? Remember, you said he dropped off the face of the earth."

I could hardly believe this was happening. "Yeah, I vaguely remember saying that. And at the time, it was true."

"So you let him waltz back into your life like nothing happened? Sorry if I have a problem with that."

"It's not for you to have a problem with! It's my life and my situation."

"Well, sorry if I had a hard time sitting there pretending to be buddies with him. I don't like it when people I care about get treated that way."

I could barely keep up. People he cared about?

"It was all a misunderstanding. Even so, we're not together. We're not a couple. It just so happened that he had a break in his schedule for the first time in a long time, and he decided to spend a few days here. Nothing more than that. And why am I even defending myself to you? I don't owe anybody an explanation."

"You're right. You don't. If you'll excuse me, I have to go wash off the yoga." He stalked away, and this time I didn't bother following. Not only had we attracted a little attention—unwanted, obviously. But he could take a walk into the ocean and never come out as far as I was concerned just then.

The nerve of him!

I got my things at the café and shook my head when it looked like Mom wanted to ask questions. "I can't. I need to go home and shower, anyway. I'm sorry I can't stick around to help out."

"I have it under control," she assured me. "So long as you're all right."

"Raina's at the apartment with Lola. If I need to talk, she'll listen." I kissed her cheek and dragged my feet out the door and down the sidewalk.

The nerve of both of them. Neither of them owned me. I didn't owe either anything.

So why did it feel like I did?

Was Joe starting to feel something more than friendship? He'd referred to me as somebody he cared about. How deep did that go? I cared about him, but as a friend.

Right?

"You have nothing to feel bad about." Raina was on the floor playing with Lola as I paced the apartment and fretted. "Deke keeps you guessing all the time, and if Joe thinks of you as more than a friend, he should say so."

I squeezed my eyes tightly shut. Raina didn't know about his past. Nobody did except for me. It wasn't my story to tell, how his wife was killed in that hit-and-run accident. For somebody who'd suffered that sort of tragedy, it wouldn't be as simple as admitting feelings for a person.

Even then, admitting feelings was never simple.

If he had started to develop feelings for me, it would've meant daring to take a chance again. There I was, clueless, assuming he would never see me as anything more than a pal, a somewhat annoying presence. All because he'd been hurt so badly, because he'd suffered so much.

Not to mention the fact that I did flat-out annoy him at times.

"It's not so easy for some people," I settled on saying.

"Sometimes, something so terrible happens that you can't bring yourself to say those sorts of things. Did I miss a sign somewhere?"

"Well, the man did yoga with you today. He doesn't strike me as the yoga type. But he made the effort. Whether or not that was for you, I don't know. But it tells me he's willing to make an effort for your sake."

I waved a hand, shaking my head. "Please. He probably figured I would never let him live it down if he didn't at least try."

"Sure, keep telling yourself that."

"Whose side are you on?"

She looked up, brows lifting. "I wasn't aware there were sides to be on. If there's a side, I'm always on yours. You know that."

I flopped down on the couch, gratified by the way Lola jumped up to be next to me. A few kisses on the cheek brought a smile to my face. "Sometimes I wish I were you," I admitted. "Life is so much simpler."

Raina snickered. "Sure, as long as she has her toys and her treats—"

In a flash, Lola launched herself off the couch and started dancing in circles.

I looked at Raina, shaking my head. "You know better."

She got up to procure said treat for my insane dog, and Lola's little treat dance couldn't have come at a better time. Laughing over her gave me the chance to reset my thoughts. "Oh! I forgot to tell you. Mrs. Merriweather was friends with Millicent!"

"You're kidding!"

"I really hope I'm as sharp as she is when I get to be her age. She is amazing." I gave her a rundown on what I'd learned.

"So Frank was the gardener's son?" Raina leaned over the counter, her chin in her palms. "Do we think a really wealthy girl would get herself involved with a guy who had absolutely no money?"

"If she did, the way Mrs. Merriweather talked about Millicent's father tells me he wouldn't have been a fan."

"But he went to Frank. Frank was the one who walked away."

"I know. Maybe this isn't the same Frank. But she swears she doesn't remember anybody other than that one, particular Frank. But Millicent could have hidden somebody from her."

"Did you say anything about the baby?"

"Well, I still don't know absolutely for sure that Millicent was the one in that picture. Maybe I can show it to her, ask her if she can identify the pregnant girl."

"Yeah, but what if Mrs. Merriweather never knew she was pregnant? That might come as a shock."

"Now that you mention it, she did say something about Millicent's father sending her to Philadelphia at one point. It meant missing Mrs. Merriweather's wedding, which she sounded really sad about. How much do you want to bet that trip to Philadelphia was a way of hiding the pregnancy and birth?"

"Maybe not the pregnancy," Raina pointed out. "She's pretty pregnant in that picture, and she's standing in front of the house here in Cape Hope."

"Oh, that's a good point. Well, maybe kept her confined to the grounds. He sounded like a real control freak. Maybe he wanted to, I don't know, be around to make sure she was healthy? Maybe he didn't want word getting out in Philadelphia if people saw her walking around like that?"

"I'll tell you, after some of the stories I've heard about what went down in my grandparents' times, I'd go with the latter explanation. He would've wanted to keep it a secret. People would talk if they saw her out there, and he never would've known she was being careful unless he saw it with his own two eyes."

I tented my fingers under my chin. "So all we really need to do right now is confirm Millicent is the one in the picture. Maybe I can take a picture of her face with my phone and show that to Mrs. Merriweather, so she won't see the belly."

This idea got two thumbs up. "Genius. You're a genius."

Was I? After missing the signals Joe might or might not have been sending my way?

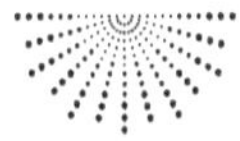

CHAPTER FOURTEEN

"I don't want to talk about it," I called out as I entered the café less than two hours after I'd left. Raina was with me, along with Lola.

"I wouldn't dream of asking," Mom called out in response. Raina snorted behind her hand, seeing this for the falsehood it was.

I went behind the counter pulled out two slices of carrot cake. "I hope one of those is for Raina," Mom chided.

"No, I planned on falling face-first into them all by myself." I stuck my tongue out at my mother as I placed one of the slices in front of Raina, who had taken a seat. It was early afternoon, the rush having died out long since.

The door to the restroom opened, revealing Trixie Graham. Auntie Trixie was in the middle of drying her hands on a paper towel. The moment she saw me, she hurried over. "Two men fighting over you?" She breathed, all excitement.

I glared at my mother, who made a point of busying

herself. "Nobody's fighting over me," I whispered. "Please, do your best not to spread that rumor."

"From what I heard, it certainly sounds like they're fighting."

I raised my voice, glaring at the familiar woman behind the counter. "Well, whoever you heard that from is completely wrong and needs to learn to mind her own business."

Mom shrugged. "I'm sorry, but it's interesting to me. They're both so handsome!"

"Yeah, well, look where that got me. It doesn't really matter, does it? Neither of them are speaking to me right now."

Since I was desperate to change the subject, I turned my attention back to Trixie. "Hey, do you remember writing those articles after Millicent Mountbatten died? Questioning what happened to her money, since nobody ever heard about where it went?"

"Sure, and I never did find any answers. No matter how many times I asked that lawyer of hers what was taking so long to settle the estate."

"Bernard Lewis."

"Right. I practically camped out in front of his house, but he refused to answer."

"All the way up in Philadelphia?"

"No, silly. Here. His summer home. Well, not strictly a summer home, since he often spends time here throughout the year. I can't believe you don't know him."

"I can't know everybody," I murmured, lost in thought. "So he wouldn't tell you anything."

"Not a thing. Not even whether she'd left her fortune to an individual, an organization. None of it. It was all very hush-hush."

"What sort of feeling did you get about him?"

She snickered, adjusting her bright red glasses. "I don't think you're old enough to hear that sort of language, young lady."

Raina burst out laughing. "There's a ringing endorsement."

I wasn't laughing. "Do you think I could go down to the courthouse and find her will there? Has enough time passed that the public can read it?"

"That would depend upon whether the estate was settled or not. If it's still in probate after all these years, the answer would most likely be no. It isn't public record until everything's finalized, as far as I know." She nodded before I had the chance to ask the question. "Yes, I checked at the courthouse, too. But it was a long time ago. Things might have changed."

Hmm. That was worth thinking about.

Mom brought a special baked good over for Lola to enjoy. "No blueberries this time," she was quick to assure me, both of us remembering what I not so fondly thought of as Lola's blue period, aka the time mom fed her enough blueberry muffins to make her poo blue for days.

At least she was little, which meant her poo was small, but still.

Trixie raised a knowing eyebrow. "What are you so interested in this for?" she asked.

"Why? Do you think there's a story in it for you?" I teased.

"Maybe. What are you thinking?" She pulled over a chair and went so far as to pick up my fork and take a bite of my carrot cake. Only a very small handful of people in the entire world could get away with that and live to tell the tale.

"I'm thinking there might be something in that will of hers that will unlock an entire puzzle. I'm not a hundred percent sure yet that I have all the pieces in order, but I'm hoping that will change soon."

It was like magic. The bell rang over the front door, and in walked Mrs. Merriweather. "Sylvia, did I leave my gloves here this morning? I traced my steps but can't seem to find them anywhere."

Mom hurried behind the counter and reached down, then straightened with a pair of mesh gloves in hand. "You took them off here at the counter, and I didn't see them until after you'd left."

"Oh, thank goodness. I was starting to doubt whether I'd worn them at all today!" She chuckled at herself as she put them on. I practically knocked my chair over, I was in such a hurry to get up.

"Mrs. Merriweather, I have a picture here on my phone. Can you tell me if it looks like somebody you know?" Just like I'd suggested to Raina, I had taken a picture of a picture. Nothing below the girl's chest was visible. I expanded it, making the face bigger so she could see.

She squinted a little, tilting her head to the side. "My goodness. Where did you find this?"

"It's a long story. Mom thinks it looks like—"

"Millicent. It's Millicent Montbatten. Is that why you were asking me about her earlier today?"

My knees went weak. Finally, I had confirmation. "Yes, that's why. I found this picture of her tucked into a used book, and I wanted to know who the girl was. Now I know."

"Wasn't she lovely? Such a good friend. I do miss her. But, that's the way of life. When you get to be my age, you miss a lot of things."

Mom drew her into conversation, while I returned to the table and sat down. I was trembling. "And now we know."

"What do we know?" Trixie asked, leaning in. I knew that look in her eye. She sensed something big was on the horizon.

I handed my phone over. "The girl in the picture is pregnant. I want to know what happened to that baby, and whether that baby was who she left her estate to. The house got sold, but that's all we ever heard of it. Right?"

"Right." Trixie's eyes narrowed. "What if it was all settled in secret?"

"It could've been. I don't know why it matters so much to me, but I need to know. Something in this world has to make sense. Something has to have a neat, tidy ending."

"Maybe she instructed her lawyer to just make a big bonfire of money and burn it," Raina shrugged. "Maybe she left it all to a favorite pet."

"While I can see myself leaving my nonexistent fortune to Lola, wouldn't that make news?" I looked at Trixie.

"Sure, it would. And that wasn't the case. She didn't even

have pets. Her favorite charities got a little something; I followed up on that, knowing she was a regular supporter of several local organizations. The bulk of her fortune went unaccounted for."

I thought about that unfinished letter she never sent. Thought about that girl. Why she captured my imagination the way she did, I had no idea. I simply had to know if everything worked out for her, for her child.

"You feel like putting your investigative skill to good use?" I asked Trixie.

She flashed a wide smile. "Always."

"Find out what happened to Frank Welburn. I have the feeling he's the key to a lot of this."

"He could be long gone by now," Raina mused, licking cream cheese frosting from her fork with a blissful expression that ran counter to the glum reality she'd just suggested.

"That's true. But, it's worth following up on." I gave Trixie the lowdown on why we thought Frank was so important. By the time I finished she was practically salivating.

"What a juicy story," she mused. "An unwed mother, forced to give up her secret baby. A baby who might've grown up to be a millionaire."

"Maybe. We don't know that yet," I reminded her.

"Which is why I said they might've." She hopped up from her chair. "Good enough. I'll start sleuthing. I've been dying to sink my teeth into something really good. Somebody didn't want me to write about a certain murder at a certain resort in a certain city not far from here."

I rolled my eyes. "And I thank you for that. I've told you so. Many times."

"I know. I just like hearing it again."

I had to laugh as she sashayed from the café. With Trixie on the case, there was no doubt we'd figure things out.

My laughter died when my phone, still sitting on the table, buzzed. "Oh, crap." I tilted it in Raina's direction so she could see Joe had texted.

"What's he say?" she whispered, craning her neck to read the message.

Just one message, short and to the point. "I acted like an idiot."

We looked at each other. She shrugged. "Yeah. He did. What else is new?"

"This is his way of apologizing. He's not big on putting that sort of thing into words and if you for one second think I'll allow you to tell me I understand him too well—"

"I wouldn't dream of it," she gasped, a hand over her chest, her lashes fluttering in mock innocence.

"Smarty pants," I muttered before typing a message in reply. *I know. I'm pretty good at that, myself.*

CHAPTER FIFTEEN

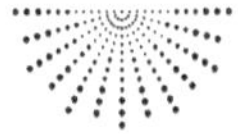

"Thank you for coming to do this with me."

"I'm still not quite sure why you need me..." Joe shot me a puzzled look.

"You're a cop. You're, I don't know, official."

"Hang on a second." He stopped dead in the middle of the sidewalk, which was inconvenient seeing as how there were people behind him at the time. They walked around him, shooting dirty looks, but he didn't seem to notice. "I'm not going to throw my job title around just because you have a whim about something."

"I wouldn't call this a whim, for one thing. And for another thing, you make it sound like I'm using you."

All he did was raise his eyebrows, which both shamed and angered me. "I'm not! Jeez Louise. If I was going to buy a car, and I wanted to bring my father with me because I knew that in our patriarchal society a man is taken more seriously when it comes to things like that—and there's less chance of them being overcharged—would you accuse me of using my father?"

"No."

I nodded. "I feel like, first off, you'll be taken more seriously than I will. And if we still get pushback from the clerk, who probably doesn't want to be working on a Saturday morning in the first place so he'll probably be in a bad mood, maybe you could casually mention that you're a detective. You don't have to pretend you're working on a case. He'll just assume."

"You know, you talk about a patriarchal society, but you assume the clerk will be a man."

"And if they happen to be a woman, we're good to go. Women tend to have a hard time refusing you, in case you didn't notice." I continued walking toward the courthouse, which was another couple blocks ahead.

"Do they?" It wasn't really a question. More of a challenge. "How so? I've never noticed."

"Oh, you are such a liar!"

"No, I'm not."

I took a big step away from him, putting a few feet between us. "Just in case lightning happens to come down and strike you where you stand, I want to make sure I don't get caught up in it."

"I'm not lying!"

"Then you're completely oblivious. Now, mind you, it's not your fault. I don't think you're willfully being oblivious to your effect on some women. Were you, like, an inordinately handsome child? Were people always commenting on how good-looking you were?" He scowled a little, and I knew I was right. "So it's just the way you've always been. You take it for granted. Believe me, try walking in the world looking like a normal person and see how far that gets you."

"How would you know?" he snickered.

"Please. There's nothing special about me. Raina is gorgeous. Men fall at her feet. I'm the one who helps them stand up again. That's the way it's always been, ever since college. She was the pretty friend."

Whatever he thought about this, he kept it to himself. "Before we go in there and make fools of ourselves, why's it so important that you see this will?"

"If that money didn't go where it was supposed to go, there's been an injustice. Maybe it did, maybe the lawyer settled things without putting any names out into the press. Maybe Millicent wanted it that way. Maybe she was still carrying those old-fashioned feelings inside—you know what I mean, like the whole baby thing had to be a secret, still. She might have specifically requested her lawyer use discretion. No big deal."

"There you go again," he chuckled.

"There I go again what?"

"Trying to save the world. You never knew this woman, you don't know her kid, but you want to make sure justice was served."

"Well, I don't consider that a fault," I sniffed.

"I never said it was." We jogged up the steps to the courthouse together, with Joe holding the door for me. "Just try not to get your hopes up too far, in case this all amounts to nothing."

"There's that positive attitude." I smirked. "It would be

like a day without sunshine."

"Cute." He followed me to the desk, where a middle-aged man I vaguely recognized eyed us suspiciously.

"Can I help you?" He might as well have yawned right in our faces.

Still, I kept a sunny disposition. "I hope so! I was wondering if I could obtain a copy of a will. I'm... doing research now that the Montbatten home is being turned into a museum, and it came to my attention that the contents of Millicent Montbatten's will were never made public. It would really be helpful to my research if I could find out where she directed her state." Where all of that came from, I had no idea. I'd walked into the courthouse with absolutely no excuse in mind.

Probably something I should've thought out before we arrived.

The man sniffed like he smelled something funny. "Oh? Do you think it's that simple? You think you're owed a look at another person's last will and testament just because you're curious?"

"Uh, yes? I'm not trying to be disrespectful, and I understand you have a job to do. But so do I." He didn't need to know that was a lie. I only hope Joe wouldn't give me away. He'd managed to keep his mouth shut so far, but there was no telling how long that would last.

A look his way from the corner of my eye told me he found this entire situation pretty funny. I should've guessed.

"You're not some disgruntled relative, are you?"

I chuckled. "Believe me, I think I would know if I was a relative. You know me. My mom runs *Sweet Nothings*? I worked there all the time. I know I've seen you in there before."

His gaze softened, just a little. Memories of Mom's baked goods tended to do that to people. "Oh, sure. And your father is Detective Harmon."

"That's right!" Good, good, this was all going well.

"I would think you would know, then, that there are certain channels a person has to go through in order to obtain a copy of another person's will. Especially when they are neither the deceased's legal counsel, nor the executor."

Son of a gun. Was he bluffing? I didn't have the foggiest idea. All I knew was, my chances of getting a look at Millicent's last wishes was dwindling with every breath I took.

"Maybe I could take a look, then," Joe suggested. I could've been imagining things, but his voice had suddenly gone deeper. More commanding. He was in full-on detective mode. "Detective Joe Sullivan, Paradise City Police Department. I'm assisting Miss Harmon in her research."

The clerk was visibly surprised by this—still, he wasn't completely convinced. "What does Paradise City have to do with this? Why would the police be investigating?"

"That's not exactly public information," Joe murmured, lowering his brow. "In honesty, I'm not operating in an official capacity. This is more of a favor to a friend. And it would go a long way toward helping us with our research if you would do us a solid. No one has to know you were involved."

The poor guy. He didn't know which end was up. A quick glance back and forth between the two of us told me he was trying to decide whether we were on the level. "You have five minutes. Five minutes from the time I bring you the document. You are not to touch it except to flip the pages, and I will be watching the entire time. No taking pictures, no nothing."

"Done! I mean, whatever you want." I was too excited to even control the volume of my voice. It rang out like the gong of bells in the otherwise empty front office. It seemed like there weren't that many people doing business there on a Saturday morning in the middle of summer.

"Okay. Wait here. Don't make me regret this." He took a set of keys with him, his footsteps clicking smartly down the hall until he disappeared into a room near the end.

I turned to Joe and clapped my hands silently. "That was great. You did a terrific job!"

"You're pretty quick on your feet." He snickered.

"If I didn't know any better, I would think that was a compliment."

"Good thing you know better, then." He rubbed the back of his neck, chagrined smile tugging the corners of his mouth. "I hope I don't end up regretting this."

"What is there to regret?"

"The fact that I name-dropped an entire police department."

I shook my head. "You walked it back pretty well. You said you weren't here in any official capacity. So you couldn't get in trouble. If you need me to back you up, I will."

"I know that's supposed to make me feel better, but…"

"Don't even say it," I warned, holding up my clenched fist.

It was only another minute or two before the clerk came back holding a folder. He was shaking his head, muttering to himself like this was a bad idea and he should've known better. I tried my best to put on a sunny smile, to reassure him somehow.

"Thank you so much," I whispered when he reached us. He very pointedly ignored my gratitude, spreading the folder open on the ledge in front of his desk.

"Remember. Five minutes, no picture taking. I have my eye on you." He took his seat, folding his arms over his chest and staring at us.

I skimmed as quickly as possible, my brain stumbling over some of the bigger words. I didn't have time to get caught up in trying to make sense of the legalese. I only wanted to know the names of her beneficiaries.

Sure enough, there was a list of organizations and charities, just like Trixie said. Considering the size of the donations—ten thousand here, twenty there—it shouldn't have comprised more than a small fraction of her overall wealth.

"A little under a half a million bucks," Joe murmured, reading along with me.

"You added that up in your head?"

"What, you think I'm incapable of basic math?" He flipped the page, and we kept reading. My eyes darted back and forth so fast, it was amazing that I hadn't given myself a headache.

Finally, we reached the last section, where the remaining

bulk of Millicent's estate was directed to a single beneficiary.

"I knew it," I whispered, my heart in my throat. "I just knew it!"

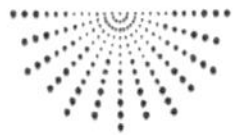

CHAPTER SIXTEEN

"Okay. So let's get this straight." Raina walked with her arms folded, which was generally how she walked when she was deep in thought. "Millicent had a son."

"She refers to him as her son in the will, yeah." I could hardly keep my heart from pounding right out of my chest. Never had I imagined getting so lucky.

"She never learned his name and had no idea where he'd ended up."

"Right."

"Or if he was even alive."

"Obviously."

"And she wanted her lawyer, this Bernard guy, to track the son down and grant him the bulk of her estate."

"Exactly. She even put his birthdate in there. August twentieth, nineteen forty-nine."

She whistled. "Not exactly ancient, but anything could've happened to the guy."

"I know. There's hope, though. Seventy isn't exactly ancient."

"No, but that's a lot of years."

"I know, I know. Come on! Aren't you excited? We're closer than ever!"

She giggled, but I had the feeling it was mostly because Lola was mirroring my energy and jumping around, pawing at my knees. That was as high up as she could reach.

"Yeah, I'm excited. I'm glad you know you're on the right track."

"We. You're just as much a part of this as I am."

We kept walking down the boardwalk, which wasn't easy with so many people around and with Lola wanting to meet every last one of them. Raina was quiet for a while before murmuring, "This isn't my mystery. Your mysteries can't always be mine. I'm gonna have to leave again, Monday morning at the latest. I promised Nate I'd visit."

"Of course! I'm not saying you have to hang around and wait for the conclusion to this. I'm sorry, did I give you the impression that you did?"

She shook her head, shrugging. "I don't know what my problem is. It's just that you've always got something going on. You have things to be enthusiastic about. I've never been good at that. If anything, I spend a lot of my time looking for things to be interested in. But I don't always find them. You're an enthusiast, and it's easy to get caught up in the things you're enthusiastic over. But they're not my things. This isn't my thing."

"Oh, sweetie." I gave her as good a hug as I could, considering I was trying to keep Lola from running off with a guy wearing skates. "You're right. And we were supposed to be hanging out this weekend, relaxing. Instead I have you wrapped up in my latest enthusiasm. Or obsession. Joe would call it that."

"Don't get me wrong, it's fun. I'm such a sucker for your little adventures. At least this one doesn't run the risk of getting you injured." She glanced at my newly unbandaged wrist. "How's it feeling?"

"Fine. Like nothing ever happened." Like I wasn't almost shot. Okay, she had a point. Sometimes I took too many chances.

"Now, as long as we can get through this without finding out the lawyer killed the son so he could keep all the money, everything will be okay."

"Oh, don't even start!" I laughed.

"So, where is Detective Joe? You said he went with you to the courthouse."

"Yeah, and he had other things to do. You're right, I have a tendency to pull people into my situations. Besides, he doesn't need to be with me all the time, does he?"

If she heard a defensive note in my voice, she was kind enough to ignore it. "You two are talking. That's good. It's never easy, when you have feelings for somebody and they only see you as a friend."

"Oh, my God. Please, don't tell me he has feelings. You're the one who always tells me not to jump to conclusions."

"Emma, I think it's time you get honest with yourself and stop pretending there's nothing between you guys. You mention him all the time, for no real reason. You just name dropped him a few minutes ago, out of nowhere. Sure, you didn't get along well at first, but that was understandable. Now, it seems like you keep finding a way to each other. He could've taken a vacation anywhere, and he came here. What's that tell you?"

"Deke could have gone anywhere else, too."

"That's true. And he chose to be here, too. You might as well face it, girlie."

"Face what?"

"No matter what you think about yourself, no matter how you brush aside people who tell you you're smart and funny and beautiful, that doesn't make it untrue. Both of these men find you super attractive, and I don't blame them. You might have been the shy, quiet girl growing up. You might've been the girl who spent most of her time either reading a book or working behind the counter. You might have been easy to overlook. But that's not the case now. And as we both know, Landon was a complete idiot to mess up what he had with you."

"Idiot being the nicest word I can think of," I muttered.

"But hey, he did you a favor. Now, you have guys he only wishes he could be half as hot and kind and successful as practically drooling over you."

I couldn't help it. I knew that what she was saying came from a good place, that she loved me, but it still made me comfortable to think of myself as anything special. She was right. I was always the girl working, reading, baking. Boys, then men, tended to overlook me.

It was so easy to assume all the men in my life wanted to be friends, because that was the way it had been for so long.

"I'm a grown woman practically in my late twenties, and I still can't get a handle on this whole situation."

"I don't think any of us ever does," she confessed. "You remember how depressed I was in Rome, during the whole Paolo situation. I'm not exactly proud of myself when I remember how everything turned around when Nate got in touch with me." Yes, even gorgeous, wealthy, jet-setting girls like Raina had insecurities.

It was easy to change the subject to happier, more pleasant things thanks to being on the boardwalk. Kids and adults alike played games in the arcade. Music floated our way from inside dozens of shops. People on the beach flew kites, played frisbee and catch. Kids squealed and splashed in the waves. The smell of so much delicious food just about drove me crazy. Which went double for poor Lola, who seemed to have developed a bad habit of begging perfect strangers for some of their food.

"I'm going to have to send her to obedience school if this keeps up," I fretted, pulling her away from a couple and their shared funnel cake. "She's too spoiled."

"How could she not be? You take one look at that little face and you want to give her everything in the whole wide world. It's her built-in defense mechanism."

"And she uses it beautifully," I laughed as my incorrigible little dog tried to sneak a french fry from an innocent passerby.

"Uh-oh. Deke Bellingham, twelve o'clock." Before I knew it, Raina had worked the leash from my hand. "He's already seen you."

"Good for him. I'm not trying to hide or run away." Still,

my legs were little shaky as I left Lola with Raina and approached him. At least he wore an easy smile, which I took as a good sign. As always, he wore his uniform of a button-down and jeans. Even in nearly ninety-degree weather. He didn't look the least bit overheated.

"Hey." His hands made it on my shoulders, but he didn't draw me in for a hug. Instead, he sighed with his mouth pulling back in a grimace. "I'm sorry. I was a jerk yesterday."

"I said some pretty harsh things, too."

"I needed to hear them. I needed a little time to think. You're right. I've been taking for granted that you would be here waiting for me, and we both know that's just not possible. How about we just try to enjoy the time we have together. I'm not trying to monopolize you, trust me."

How could I look up at that smile and those gold-flecked eyes without melting a little? "We were just taking a walk. You should join us." I took his hand and led him back to Raina, who greeted him warmly.

But he saved most of his warmth for Lola, crouching in front of her and scratching behind her ears. "Her breath smells like french fries," he announced, looking up at me.

Raina looked at Lola. Lola looked at Raina. They both looked at me. "She really wanted one," Raina shrugged. "What was I supposed to do when the kid gave it to her? Take it out of her mouth?"

I shrugged. "If it upsets her stomach, you're the one cleaning up after her tonight. That's all I have to say."

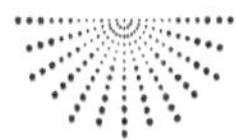

CHAPTER SEVENTEEN

I could only hope Bernard Lewis wouldn't have me arrested for stalking or loitering or whatever.

Were people ever arrested for loitering? Probably not. Maybe just ticketed. Did I want a ticket? No, especially since that would mean my father finding out about my hanging out in front of his house, waiting for him to come out.

"Trust me," Trixie had assured me when we spoke on the phone. "He always goes for breakfast at the diner on Sunday mornings. I've seen him there more times than I can count."

"You mean you have breakfast somewhere other than at the café?" I'd teased. "I'll be sure not tell Mom about it."

"You're a troublemaker," she'd reminded me.

"Takes one to know one."

So, here we were, Lola and I. Sitting on a bench near the curb across from Mr. Lewis's house. I must've passed it a thousand times in my life. A three-story Victorian on a corner lot, pale blue trimmed in white with a wrap-around porch. The lawn was emerald green, the sign of somebody who had the money to cover a really good lawn service.

"Do you have business to do?" I asked Lola in a soft voice. "Did those french fries stop you up? That's what you get, you stinker. Here I was, thinking you'd have the opposite problem after your little boardwalk buffet. Auntie Raina got off lucky. I'm convinced you two have been plotting against me."

The house looked completely quiet. No big surprise, seeing as how it was barely eight in the morning. He lived there with his wife, according to Trixie. She tended to know random things like that.

If I didn't know better, I'd think we were related by blood.

"Knowing my luck, this will be the one Sunday he decides to skip out on breakfast."

Lola looked up at me. There was nothing she could do about it, clearly, though I couldn't help wishing there was.

There was a car in the driveway, so at least that was a good sign. He hadn't gone out early.

It wasn't like I couldn't come back at a later time. Why did it feel so urgent? Why did I have to do it right this very minute? Patience was never my strong suit.

And he could spend his entire week in Philly and not come back until the following weekend, and I couldn't possibly wait all week. I'd die from the suspense. It would be easier to get an answer from him on the street than it would if I visited his office. I didn't need to go through the humiliation of being asked to leave his high-priced law firm's main office to know how it would go.

Thus, waiting outside his house to attack him when he least suspected was the best course of action.

"I'm only gonna ask a few questions," I explained to my dog, though clearly she couldn't possibly have cared less. It was way more important to her that she sniff the ground, the base of the tree we sat near. "Oh, sorry. I didn't mean to interrupt while you're checking your messages from the other dogs in the neighborhood."

She looked up at me just before squatting to leave a little message of her own.

"Charming. Sometimes I think you understand me much better than you should."

Moments later, the door to the Lewis house opened. It was quiet enough on the street that I heard the latch release from all the way on the opposite sidewalk. I darted across with Lola trotting faithfully at my side.

"Mr. Lewis?" I called out as he walked down the pathway between the front steps and the sidewalk.

"Yes?" He squinted at me from underneath the brim of his ball cap. "Can I help you?"

"Sorry to blindside you like this," I laughed, a little breathless from the short run. I really did need to start working out.

"It's all right, I assume." He checked his Rolex.

"We can talk and walk," I suggested. "I know my friend here wants to walk."

He grinned down at Lola. "She's sweet. But I'm still not entirely sure I want to talk to you. What's this all about?"

The man appeared to be in his early sixties. I knew from my internet digging that he was a sharp cookie who managed the estates of several clients with high net worths. If people with names like theirs trusted him, he had to know what he was doing.

I'd have to be smart about this, in other words. This wasn't an underpaid clerk who had nothing better to do on a Saturday morning than help me out. I couldn't wave the word "detective" around in his face and expect him to stand at attention, either.

So, charm it was.

I gave him the whole smile, full teeth and everything. "I'm doing a little research into one of the town's prominent citizens. Late citizens, that is. Millicent Montbatten."

"Oh, certainly. Millie was a great lady. Come on, walk with me. I have a standing breakfast date with a few friends."

Excellent. Lola was happy to trot slightly ahead of us as we went. He had a quick stride—places to go, people to see—and I adjusted my pace to keep up with him.

"Millie—I called her Millie, she insisted—was very kind. Generous. A member of the old school, if you will." He chuckled softly. "I was her lawyer for fifteen years before she allowed me to call her Millie. Even then, I nearly choked every time I used the nickname. She was a powerful person with a quick wit and a strong personality. If she wanted things done a certain way, that's simply the way it was."

Yet he'd boxed up her treasured books and dumped them in Darcy's lap, hadn't he? Silly me, it probably hadn't been him. He'd more than likely hired a company to handle it.

"She didn't have any family left by the time she passed

on, did she? I was away at school when that happened, but I remember what a big deal it was. I guess just about everything that happens around here is a big deal by default."

His laugh boomed out in the otherwise quiet morning. "You have a way with words."

"I'm a writer," I shrugged. "And no, I don't think I've written anything you might've heard of."

"You get that question a lot?"

"Sometimes." We exchanged a smile. "So you knew Millicent well?"

"Very well. I might've been the closest person to her, in the end."

"That's pretty close for a lawyer. One wouldn't expect their lawyer to be so close to them."

"I guess I felt sorry for her." He was kind enough to pause while Lola went all-in on sniffing a tree trunk like her life depended on it. "She didn't have anybody else. Her last few years were spent solely in that monstrosity of a house. Her food was delivered, the household staff saw to her needs. That was hardly the same as having friends."

I couldn't help wondering if he'd angled to get himself included in the will. Was I jaded? He might've been a nice guy who felt sorry for an old woman who didn't have anyone else in her life. Was that a crime all of a sudden?

"It's nice that she had somebody in the end who cared about her needs." I cleared my throat. We were coming to the uncomfortable part. And with little time to spare, since the diner was only a couple of blocks away. I could see the unlit, chrome-trimmed sign already.

"Somebody had to."

"What about her son? How did he feel when he found out who his mother was?"

Maybe I could've gone about that in a better way. Maybe I didn't have to drop it in his lap like a ticking bomb. Maybe Mom was right all those times she'd accused me of liking drama too much.

He stopped in his tracks. "What did you just say?"

I turned to him. The look of slack-jawed wonder was clear even though his face was shaded.

"Her son. The son she mentioned in her will as her primary beneficiary. The son whose name she never learned. He was given up for adoption, wasn't he? I mean, I imagine he was."

"What gives you the right—"

"I only want to know if he got what was left him, whoever he is. That's all. There was never a word of it in the paper, nobody in town knows. It was a mystery for a long time. Nobody ever found out who he was—I mean, nobody even knows he exists except for me and a few others."

"How dare you?"

"How dare I what? Why does this have to be such a huge secret? It's not the forties anymore. It isn't like I plan on going to the newspaper and telling them she had a baby out of wedlock. If anything, anybody who read the story would want to know her son got what she wanted for him. A secure, stable life thanks to her wealth."

"It isn't any of your affair, young woman, and I would appreciate it if you'd let me go about my day in peace." He tried to get past me, but neither Lola nor I would let him get away that easily. She ran around him in a circle, tangling him in the leash. "Damn it!" he growled.

"Calm down. I'll untangle you." I walked around him to unwind the leash, but I took my time about it.

"Hurry up!"

"Why can't you tell me whether or not you found her son? That was your job, wasn't it? She wanted you to find him, because she trusted you."

"It's none of your concern, that's why. It's a private matter."

"So you won't say yes or no? You can't even do that much? I'm not asking for a name, Mr. Lewis." I finished untangling him, silently reminding myself to give Lola an extra treat when we got home.

"I refuse to be badgered this way." He tried to push me out of the way this time, and he came close to getting what he wanted. I stumbled back, landing against a parked car.

"How dare you put your hands on me?" I shouted. It took a lot to get me worked up, but minor physical assault was right up there at the top of the list of things that made me furious.

"How dare you stick your nose into business that has nothing to do with you?"

"You do realize I could hire a lawyer and find out with their help just what happened to Millicent's money, right? Whether you saw it turned over to its rightful owner. Or if you were just too lazy and jealous that somebody else got something you thought you deserved to do your job!"

He sputtered, red-faced, and for a second I felt more secure. Just like at the courthouse, I hadn't planned anything that had just come out of my mouth. But it was the right instinct, because it shook him into silence.

Silence that was quickly broken by the squeal of brakes.

So many things happened at once.

I looked down.

She wasn't there.

My hand was empty.

I'd dropped the leash when I stumbled.

And Lola. Where was she?

"Lola?" I whispered, afraid to turn around and see what I knew I'd see. "Lola!"

All I heard was a soft yipping coming from the middle of the street.

CHAPTER EIGHTEEN

"I swear, I'll never forgive myself. Not ever, ever." I sat with my face in my hands, crying hard enough to take my breath away. I hadn't stopped crying since finding Lola lying in the street, nearly under the tire of the car that hit her.

"I'm sure she'll be okay," Raina whispered, rubbing my back.

"She might've had internal injuries. I have no idea. Oh, my God. My poor girl." I couldn't shake the memory of trying to pick her up. She'd let out this pitiful little whine while staring up at me with those puppy eyes.

Begging for help. Accusing me for forgetting her. I'd forgotten all about her, hadn't I? She might as well not have been there at all.

"I was too wrapped up. Yelling at that man, fighting with him. I forgot her. I let her go. What else was she gonna do without me holding on? Obviously, she'd go out in the street. I'll never forgive myself."

"She'll be fine, sweetie." Only she didn't sound like she believed it herself. She was only saying what she was supposed to say, the sort of thing people told each other when things looked awful and there was no hope. A friend would want to encourage and soothe their friend, even if they had no idea what they were talking about.

"If she dies, I won't be able to stand it. I just won't."

"Honey, dogs don't outlive us. Not most of the time."

"Please, please, I know that. But this isn't the same as her getting sick, something I can't control. This is my fault. I wasn't watching her. I might as well have pushed her into the street."

I barely remembered calling Raina. And even when I had, I was crying too hard to make much sense. The driver of the car had taken the phone from me and explained before driving us to the vet's office. It was obvious they felt terrible about the whole thing.

I couldn't even remember if it was a man or a woman. I was that out of it. All I could think about was Lola.

Though I vaguely recalled saying I wouldn't sue. It wasn't their fault.

It was mine.

The door to the back room opened. I couldn't stand up with my legs shaking the way they were.

Raina stood, though, facing the vet. "How is she?"

He smiled. "She has a broken leg, but otherwise she'll be just fine."

That should've made me happy. Instead, I sobbed harder than ever.

"We did a full x-ray just to be sure, and I didn't see any

internal damage. She must've tried to dart away when she saw the car coming and gotten clipped by a wheel. It happens all the time."

"See? She'll be fine." Raina hugged me. "She's fine."

"If you think she was spoiled before—"

"It'll be a hundred times worse now," she chuckled. "I know."

I managed to get it together enough to talk to the doctor. "Um, what's next? A cast?"

"Yes, a cast. A splint. And a cone of shame, as they call them. At least until she's accustomed to the splint. Otherwise, she'll bite at it."

"Sure, sure. I understand. But you're absolutely sure there's no other damage? No breaks or bleeding?

"I'm absolutely sure," he smiled. He seemed like a nice person, and patient. He didn't even stiffen up when I threw my arms around his neck.

"Thank you so much." I had to step back before my tears soaked into his scrubs.

"We'll get started with the cast now. It won't take long, with her being such a small dog. It should take roughly four weeks to heal. I'll bring her out to you when we're finished. Don't be surprised if she's a little slow or dull. We'll be giving her something for the pain."

"Of course. I don't want her in pain." I watched him walk away with my hands folded, thanking my guardian angels and Lola's for protecting her.

"Now that she'll have a cast, she'll be cuter than ever. I can't resist a doggie in a cast." Raina handed me a paper cup of water from the cooler near the door. "Here. Calm down, or she'll know how upset you are. Meds or no meds."

"Yeah, right. Of course." But I couldn't stop blaming myself, no matter what she or the vet or anybody said. I was a rotten idiot for letting her go. All because I was too wrapped up in what was happening with some perfect stranger, relating to the life of another perfect stranger.

She could've been killed. Easily. If she'd gone just a little further into the street, or if she'd darted in one direction instead of another, that would've been it. And I would've had to carry that with me for the rest of my life.

"Emma?"

I couldn't have been more surprised to see my father enter the office, though he was just the person I needed. I sank against him and he hugged me tight. "Honey, how is she?"

"Her leg's broken, but she'll be okay."

"Oh, thank goodness."

"How did you know?" Raina asked.

"I heard it through the grapevine. You know how it is." He pulled away, looking down at me. "Actually, Holly and I were having breakfast at the diner. Bernard Lewis came in talking about a little Maltese who was hit by a car down the street, and how the dog's owner wouldn't leave him alone about some legal issue. Tell me who that sounds like."

"Oh, jeez. That guy." I blew my nose and wiped my eyes. "What a jerk. He pushed me. That's when I dropped the leash."

"I'll kill him," Dad snarled.

"It's okay. He didn't hurt me. And it wasn't his fault I was negligent. Lola should've been my primary concern. But no, I got all wrapped up in something that isn't really all that important to me. She's what's important, not some will or secret baby."

"I would have to agree."

Raina picked up her purse. "I'll go outside and call the café. I'm sure word must've spread by now."

"Thanks," I whispered, sinking into a chair. Something told me Dad would want to speak privately. And it wouldn't be pretty.

I'd have to thank Raina later for leaving me alone with him, the sneak. Though Mom would be half out of her mind with worry by now, and a phone call was only the right thing.

"Emma." He sat next to me. "What's going on with you? Why did you accost that awful guy?"

"Awful? Why do you say that?"

"Oh, come on. Everybody knows what a jerk Bernie Lewis is."

"Well, I'm not one of those people who knows it. No, scratch that. I didn't know it before this morning."

"You have no business getting mixed up with him. Why would you approach him? What was it all about?"

"Remember when I said I found that old picture? I was talking about it with Holly the night you told me about the baby."

"Sure. The Montbatten house was in it."

"Right. It was Millicent in the picture. She had a baby years ago, but nobody knew about it. She left her money to him in her will, and I wanted to know if this Lewis guy made good on how she wanted things done. She didn't know the baby's name, only that she gave birth to a boy. That's what the will said."

"And you would know this how?"

"Because I read it."

"Emma Jane."

"What? I know, I bend the rules too much. I just wanted to know, Dad. I wanted to know her baby got what he deserved. Or his family, if he's dead. It's only right."

"I know, honey, but you can't always be the one to make these things happen. Look what it got you today. Once this situation with Millicent's money is settled, you'll still have Lola. And your own life. Your career, your friends. That's what matters. Everything else will fade to the background, just like always. Robbie Klein has gone on with his life; thanks to you, of course. Same thing with Nate, and Georgia. And I'm sure none of them will forget the way you helped them, but in the end all you're left with is your life. Yours alone. And you keep taking these risks, even when you don't know how risky they are."

"You're right. I would've wanted to die if Lola was killed today." I leaned against him. He smelled the way he always did, thanks to the aftershave he'd been using since before I was born. It was a comforting scent, something that reminded me of security and peace. I needed it just then.

"I know you would have, sweetie. I think it's time you take care of what needs taking care of in your life. I understand you've been refusing opportunities to travel for work."

"What the heck? Why does everybody know this? I'll strangle Raina."

"Don't bother. She cares about you. Sometimes, we have to trust the people around us to see the things we can't see for ourselves." He draped an arm over my shoulders. "I want you to take these opportunities."

"Mom already gave me the lecture."

"You'll get it from me, too, just to drive the point home. You have the whole world at your fingertips. Why do you think your mother and I worked so hard for so long? To give you opportunities. To provide as stable a life as we could for you and Darcy, so you could thrive."

"Is that why you stayed together for so long?"

He didn't answer right away. We had never talked about it before, not that openly. Given the topic, it seemed like a natural question.

"Yeah, that's why. Don't get me wrong, it wasn't always bad. Difficult, but marriage can be that way for anybody. We woke up one day and I realized I was looking at a stranger. We were two people with completely separate lives who just happened to share children. That was it. I never stopped caring for her, but I didn't want to live that way anymore. It didn't seem fair to either of us. Maybe you don't understand—"

"No, I do. Completely." And I wished Darcy would give him the chance to explain things for himself. She might have come around years earlier.

"I say all that to say, I want more for you than sticking around town because you feel like you have to. I know your mom doesn't want you to limit yourself, any more than I do. We both want what's best for you. That'll never change."

"I understand." I was so tired, completely wrung out, but I understood that much at least.

The door to the back room opened, and the vet—who'd be on my holiday card list until the end of time as far as I was concerned—carried Lola out to me.

"Baby! Oh, my goodness, look at your pink cast! It's almost as big as you!" Her right rear leg was the broken one, poor thing. Just like the doctor had warned, she was sort of lethargic as he handed her off to me.

"Don't worry," he murmured when I frowned down at her. "Like I said, she's drugged at the moment. This has nothing to do with how well she'll recover. You won't be able to keep up with her in a few weeks."

"I'm so sorry," I whispered into her fur. She gave me a soft, tired lick.

"Here's some information on what to do for her. And what to absolutely not do. Including medication. Animals should never get human meds, even something as simple as aspirin."

I was too busy fawning over Lola to tell him I wasn't an idiot. He handed Dad the paperwork and Lola's cone of shame. "She's too tired and drugged-out now to be curious, but that'll wear off soon. I know you'll feel badly about using it, but it's for her own good."

I thanked him roughly thirty times before we left the office. Things could've been so much worse. Every terrible thing that had gone through my head during the ride to the vet's came back to me, choking me up.

"I guess I'd better get home and give Holly the good news." Dad kissed my forehead before helping me into the passenger seat of Raina's car. "Remember what we talked about."

"I will," I promised.

He patted Lola's head before closing the door.

"Everything okay?" Raina asked once she was behind the wheel.

"Yeah, just fine. Everything's fine." I nuzzled Lola, knowing how lucky we both were.

Maybe it was time for me to take a step back and evaluate, the way Dad said. My personal life was in shambles, I had opportunities to travel—even though I'd hate to leave Lola, I knew she'd be in good hands.

I had to stop caring so much about my personal projects. The people who needed my help. I needed my help, too.

And I told myself this. I really did, the entire way to Mom's café.

Even as, in the back of my head, I knew there was a man out there who had no idea he was a millionaire.

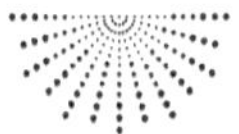

CHAPTER NINETEEN

"There she is!" Mom ran across the café and practically ripped Lola from my arms.

"Careful," I warned. It was hard to keep myself calm. I only managed it for the dog's sake. "We have to be careful with her leg."

"Of course, we do. You don't need to tell me that." She peppered the dog's head with kisses. "Goodness, I considered shutting down the café. I was that upset."

"Well, I'm glad you didn't. Besides, I would've needed somewhere to go if the worst had happened."

"Don't even think such a thing," she advised. She touched my face, eyes narrowing as she studied me. "And how are you? How are you holding up?"

"Oh, about the same as you'd expect. I want to crawl into bed and not come out for a few days. I swear, she's the one who got hit, but I'm the one who saw my whole life flash before my eyes." I sat down, still cradling her.

And it was so clear that she loved the attention. Sick or

not, she soaked in the love and the kisses. She'd be impossible to live with after this, but I would never complain.

Raina sat across from me, removing her sun hat and shaking out her hair. "What a morning. Hopefully somebody will know better than to run out in the street after this."

"She'll never have to even think about it, because I'm not letting her out of my sight ever again."

"Now, now." Mom returned to her place behind the counter, where she started cleaning up the coffee station. "I don't want to hear that. I know you feel that way now, but you'll have to adjust to it in the future when you have a job to go to. You'll just have to trust us to take good care of her, and you know we will."

Yes, I knew Mom would take excellent care of her. My little girl might always be a little heavier than she was before I left her thanks to the abundance of treats, but she was happy and healthy. The situation was just a little too fresh, still. I couldn't bring myself to imagine being away from her.

"And if she is just not the cutest thing with that cast. It's so unfair." Raina reached over to pet Lola's head.

"What? That she looks so cute with the cast, or that she has to wear one in the first place?"

"Both," Raina laughed.

The front door burst open, and Darcy was practically on top of me before I knew it. "Oh, my God! I'm so glad she's okay!"

"Gosh, I knew news traveled quickly around here, but this is unexpected." I was still wary of my sister. Sure, this sort of thing tended to bring people together, but if she was just going to ignore me after this, I really didn't want anything to do with her. I'd been through a trauma—much more so for the dog, naturally, but this sort of thing was never easy for a pet owner, either.

"And that little cast!" Her eyes filled with tears. "Oh, my gosh. Poor baby. She must've been so scared. We're just gonna spoil you rotten, aren't we sweetheart? Yes, we are." She nuzzled Lola's head.

I stayed quiet, watching and waiting. Sure, it was moving to see her like this. Something ached in my chest, something suspiciously close to the location of my heart. But she was so mean, and so cold. I hoped she didn't think this close call changed anything, not unless she had every intention of apologizing for her behavior.

Slowly, her gaze lifted until her eyes met mine. "I'm sorry, you know. I said awful things."

"So did I," I admitted in a whisper.

"But I deserved it. I needed to hear it. I was stubborn and childish." She ran a hand under both eyes, wiping away tears.

"So was I."

"I was worse," she insisted.

"For heaven's sake, this isn't a competition. Just make up and get it over with you two." Mom shook her head. "Honestly, the two of you. I could bang your heads together. Maybe that would knock some sense into you."

"Funny, that's usually how I feel about you," I snarked.

She stuck her tongue out. I did the same thing right back. Things were back to normal.

Darcy stood with a smile. "Hang on a sec. I have something for you." She jogged out of the café and headed straight for the bookstore.

"What's that about?" Raina murmured.

I could only shrug. "How would I know? I haven't talked to her in days."

"I'm just glad you're talking again." She sighed. "I hate the idea of you guys not getting along. I feel better leaving you here on your own, knowing you have her."

"You make it sound like I don't live here, like I have nobody else."

"But it's different, having a sister. At least, I assume. I wouldn't know, as you are well aware."

"Now I feel bad, letting you run around the world without a sister along with you." I pouted.

"You could come along with me. We'll run around the world together and have adventures and leave a wake of dazed, longing men in our wake."

"Aw, but then what would I do with this girl?" I asked, pouting more than ever. I put on a high-pitched voice. "Auntie Raina, why would you do that to me?"

"Stop it," she warned, giggling.

"I would miss my mommy so much!" I squeaked. "And Grandmom would stuff me so full of you-know-what that begins with the letter T, my tummy would rub against the ground when I walked!"

"I would not!" Mom insisted. "You have no faith in me."

"No comment," I whispered before turning to Raina. "Anyway, I'm gonna take your advice. And Mom's advice.

And Dad's advice—by the way, thanks for squealing on me to him, too. That was terrific."

"I was feeling a little desperate and was very worried about you. I figured why not improve the odds that you'd actually listen to reason?"

I couldn't argue, as much as I wanted to.

Darcy came back with yet another small, old book in one hand.

I gave Lola to Raina in favor of examining it. "Another one!"

"Another one. It's crazy to think how long these books sat there, without anybody knowing what was inside." She pulled up a chair. "Look what's in the back."

Another picture. I forgot to breathe as I slid it out from between the pages.

It was Millicent again, only she wasn't alone this time. She sat on a towel on the beach, leaning against a devastatingly handsome young man. She wore a super cute, old-fashioned bathing suit with a halter neckline. Her dark hair was pulled back with a ribbon, and a pair of sunglasses sat on top of her head.

He wore a pair of bathing trunks and a wide, almost goofy smile.

He was looking at her, while she was looking at the camera.

"My God, he adored her," I whispered, staring at the couple. "They're so cute together, too."

"I know, right? I'm obsessed with them." Darcy leaned in, shaking her head. "He's so handsome."

"Like a movie star," I agreed. He had a square jaw, deep-set eyes, wavy black hair. "He reminds me of… what was his name? Tyrone something."

"Tyrone Power? Where?" Mom practically flew over to where we sat. He'd always been one of her favorites.

"It's not him, but it looks like him. Doesn't it?" I held the photo out for her to see.

"Oh, yes indeed. Mm-mm-mm." She practically licked her lips. Boy, did this woman need a man in her life.

"And he's with Millicent. I wonder if that's Frank."

"Who's Frank?" Darcy asked. Right. We hadn't been talking. I filled her in as quickly as I could while Mom doted on the dog worse than she'd already been.

"Here's the thing, though." I studied the picture again and tried to see him as the slimeball who'd walked away from his girlfriend and their unborn baby. "Does he look like somebody who was only in it for a little booty?"

"Emma!" Mom hissed, scandalized.

"Okay. This from the woman who just about salivated over a photo from seventy years ago," I muttered. "But it's the truth. I'm not making things up. She accused him of using her, and I would do the same thing in her position. She accused him of only wanting one thing out of her. When he got it, he was gone."

"It's not that easy," Mom sighed. "Imagine how frightening that could've been for him. Don't get me wrong, I think it's terrible if he deserted her. But I can also imagine how a wealthy girl's father would put an abundance of pressure on a working-class boy to do right by her, if you get what I mean."

"He probably felt like he could never measure up to the sort of life she was used to," Raina murmured.

"It's still not an excuse," I argued. "He shouldn't have run away. Even if he felt like he couldn't measure up or what have you, he didn't have to abandon her like he did."

"They might've worked things out later on," Darcy suggested. She sounded so hopeful. I could understand why; the couple in the picture looked so happy. And the boy looked like he was so much in love. I wanted to believe they'd eventually come to an understanding, too.

"Maybe. Maybe that's why Millicent never sent the letter. Maybe there was no reason to send it." I wanted to believe that, but I couldn't. It didn't feel right.

"We'll have to find out." Darcy looked around. "Right?"

"Is that how I sound when I decide I have to do something?" I muttered to Raina, who gave me a wide-eyed, dramatic nod. Maybe a little too dramatic for my liking, but whatever.

"Well?" Darcy prompted, nudging me. "I wanna know how things turned out for these two crazy kids."

"We know how things turned out for Millicent," I reminded her in a soft voice. "She passed away without ever having married, with no relatives—none that we knew of, anyway."

"Don't you want to make sure the right thing was done by her baby?"

"Sweetie, I've been worrying about that for days. I was worrying about it when I dropped Lola's leash and she was almost killed. I need to focus my priorities. This can't be it.

And you can put away the puppy dog eyes," I added when Darcy just about started whimpering.

"Fine. I'll do it myself. I'll finish what you started." Darcy stood, fists clenched. "I want to see how this played out."

"Don't be so dramatic."

"Look who's talking!" she laughed. "You! The queen of drama!"

"You need to remember that we just made up, miss lady," I grumbled, folding my arms. "I'm sorry, but I've been too wrapped up in other people's lives for too long. I need to focus on me."

The bell chimed, and in walked Trixie. "Guess what? I found Frank Welburn!"

Darcy gasped, turning to me.

Raina gasped, too.

In truth, so did I.

Dang it. Just when I thought I was out…

CHAPTER TWENTY

"I'm the only person who could do this for you at this very minute?" Joe shot me a look from behind the wheel. "Is there any reason why you couldn't drive yourself?"

"For one thing, I've been through a very trying day. If I recall correctly, I told you my dog almost died."

"And that's terrible. Seriously. I'm so glad she's okay. I'm sure that must've been awful."

"It was." I looked out the window because it was easier than letting him see my eyes welling up. "Anyway, Darcy has to mind the store. Trixie has things to do. Raina's taking care of Lola since she shouldn't be left alone right now. Mom's working, obviously."

"True, I'm sure."

"Besides, you've been with me through this. I thought maybe you'd find it interesting."

He was quiet for a minute before asking, "You're sure

you're not bringing me along so I can wave my badge around?"

"No! Jeez. I wasn't even thinking that until you said it. Honestly."

He seemed to accept this. At least, he didn't offer an argument.

"What about Deke?" he murmured.

I could barely hear him, his voice was so soft. Wonderful. He was doing this. This was actually happening.

"What about him?" I sighed. "I don't know any other way to explain this. There's nothing serious between us. We see each other every once in a while. And it just happens that right now, you're both in town at the same time. Believe me, I don't crave difficulty. It would be nice if something could be simple for once. Peaceful. Easy. Instead, I can't even ask you for a ride to the nursing home where Frank Welburn lives without getting raked over the coals."

"I'm raking you over the coals?"

"That's sure how it feels over here in the passenger seat!" I growled. "I've had an incredibly trying day and that's why I didn't trust myself to drive. I'm still shaky. And I didn't want to do this by myself. Okay? I'm not thrilled about walking around a nursing home in the first place."

"What, are you afraid?"

"I don't like that nasty tone," I whispered. "You sound very nasty right now. Like you're making fun of me."

"I'm not trying to make fun"

"You're doing a pretty good impression of somebody who's trying to make fun."

"I'm not. I mean it." He snickered. "Okay. Maybe I was sort of making fun, but gently. I was gently teasing."

"You were making fun. I'm sorry if walking through a nursing home isn't something I'm completely comfortable with. I have a lot of bad memories."

"Of your time in a nursing home?"

"I will take the wheel and steer us off the road, I swear."

"Sorry, sorry. Okay. I'll be serious. You've visited nursing homes in the past?"

"When I was little," I admitted. "My grandmom was in one. She lived with us for a little while. Mom was dead-set against sending her to a facility. That was the word she always used. A facility. Anyway, she didn't wanna do it. So when Grandmom couldn't be trusted to live alone anymore, Mom insisted she live with us."

"How did your dad feel about that?"

"He was fine with it. He agreed with her. Don't get me wrong. They got along well for a really long time. They were nice to each other. They supported each other. Especially back then."

"Got it. I guess things didn't work for long, though? Since she ended up in a facility?"

I tapped a finger to my nose. "It was around three months, I think. Maybe. I was, like, seven at the time so my timeline might be off. See, and I didn't find this out until I was older, Grandmom had suffered several small strokes. Nobody knew that until later. She was more confused than Mom thought. She woke up in the middle of the night once and thought somebody was trying to break into the house, even though there was nobody outside anywhere. It was, like, three in the morning and Dad was out there with his service weapon, checking for intruders. She was too worked up to go back to sleep that night. I think that was the straw that broke the camel's back. They weren't equipped."

"That's very sad. And common, I think," he added, sympathetic.

"I guess it is. So, we visited all the time. Just about every week. And it was… harrowing. Especially for a little kid."

"I can't imagine. And I'm sorry for making a joke out of this. Really. I wouldn't wanna go in by myself if that was how I remembered things being in the past, either."

"Thank you. And thanks for coming with me, too, I guess."

He cleared his throat, tapping his fingers on the wheel. "So. Trixie found this place."

"Yeah. I don't know how she managed it. That's what she does. She could find a needle in a haystack. He's been living in this home in Sea Harbor for the last several years."

"Wow. All this time, he wasn't that far away. A stone's throw, practically."

We arrived a few minutes later. "It looks nice," I murmured. "And huge."

"Enormous," he sighed as we drove around. "Where do we even go in? Where's the front of the place?"

"Have I been here before? I have no idea."

"It was more of a rhetorical question. I didn't expect you to answer."

"Sorry. I'm a little tense. I told you this."

"Maybe this wasn't the right day to come out to see him,"

he suggested. "We can always come back another time. Maybe tomorrow, when you're feeling better."

"Heck, no. We already came all this way. And I doubt I could get away with going home and having nothing to offer my sister. She's more obsessed with this than I am now."

The building was very clean looking, well maintained. Pretty, cheerful flowers grew all along the walkways, under the windows, in clusters around the trees which dotted the green lawn.

"This is nice. It really is." Joe sounded positive for the first time since we left. No, for the first time since I called to ask for a ride to Sea Harbor.

I got the sense he was trying his best for my sake, which both endeared him to me and made me more nervous than ever. He was being nice. So nice. What did that mean? Was I overthinking this? Yes, I was obviously overthinking it.

What was the alternative? Remembering every uncomfortable, frightening visit to Grandmom's nursing home?

It might've been safer, come to think of it.

The lobby was very pretty, with shiny floors and potted plants. High-backed wicker furniture held smiling, laughing older people. Some of them played cards and checkers while others read magazines. A few ladies clustered in a circle in one corner and knitted. "Wow," Joe breathed. "This is much better than I would've imagined. Wasn't this Frank guy supposed to be working class?"

"Maybe his situation improved over time. Lots of water under the bridge and all that." None of the men bore even a slight resemblance to the boy in the picture, though I knew that wasn't to be expected. Even if he was sitting there right then, I wouldn't have recognized him after seven decades.

"Can I help you?" A young woman in a flowered smock stopped on her way past, smiling kindly.

"Yes, my name is Emma Harmon. This is my friend, Joe Sullivan. We're here to visit one of your residents. Mr. Frank Welburn."

Recognition ignited behind her eyes. "Oh, Mr. Welburn. Sure. And you know him how?"

Shoot. Should've thought this one through. My brain was in tatters after the events of the day.

It was Joe who jumped in and saved me. "We're friendly with an old friend of his. Mrs. Merriweather, she lives down in Cape Hope. She mentioned he lived here but, you know how it is. She gets tired easily and can't drive herself, certainly. We thought it would be nice to check in on him for her."

Was it the very good, believable story that did the trick? Or was it Joe's insanely good looks? Whatever the reason, I was glad to see the girl nod in appreciation. "That's very sweet. Mr. Welburn doesn't get a lot of visitors. Just his nephew, for the most part. I'll show you to his room."

"Thanks so much!" I shot Joe a look of gratitude which he shrugged off.

We followed the girl down a maze of hallways, twisting and turning. I wondered if we'd ever find our way out. "I should've left a trail of breadcrumbs!"

"Yes, it can be confusing for first-time visitors. If you have any problems finding your way out, just ask any of us that work here."

"Good to know." Joe and I exchanged a nervous glance.

"But you do have to be careful," she warned, punching a code into a keypad before opening a metal door. "We're entering the memory care unit, and the residents who live in this wing can't wander the facility. Hence the code."

"Flight risk?" Joe asked.

"Pretty much. It's for their benefit. When you leave, be sure you're the only ones leaving."

We exchanged another look. I almost wished I could reach out and take Joe's hand. Any little bit of comfort would've been nice. His presence would have to be enough.

This section of the building wasn't quite as nice as the rest. The floors were carpeted as opposed to polished hardwood. The ceilings were lower, the halls narrower. There were signs hanging in front of some of the doors. Fall Risk was a common one.

We reached a door with Frank's name on the front. "Here we are." She knocked softly before opening the door a crack. "Frank? Mr. Welburn? You have visitors."

"Who's here to see me?" he called out. His voice was surprisingly strong and healthy, which bolstered my flagging spirits. For a second there, I was afraid he wouldn't be able to give us any information. Memory care didn't exactly inspire confidence, especially when the memories we were interested in were seven decades old.

The room was a nice size and comfortably furnished. Frank was watching a baseball game with the volume turned up practically all the way. Evidently, he didn't have the sort of high-powered hearing aid Mrs. Merriweather used.

The aide helpfully turned the volume down while I waved to Frank, who sat in an armchair.

"Who're you?" he asked, frowning.

"Now, Mr. Welburn. That's not a way to talk to visitors." She winked at Joe before leaving the room. I noticed she didn't close the door all the way. Would she listen from outside?

I had to plow ahead anyway. "My name is Emma, and this is Joe. Mr. Welburn, I live in Cape Hope. Didn't you used to live there?"

"Cape Hope?" He looked and sounded confused. My heart sank.

Until his expression cleared up. "Cape Hope! Certainly, I lived there for years. What ever made you think of old Cape Hope?"

"I… live there, as I said." I felt like I was already drowning. "Uh, do you recognize this picture?"

I handed him the picture of the couple on the beach. Another look at it, after seeing him as he currently was, told me without a doubt that he was the guy sitting with Millicent. He still had that same thick, wavy hair—some people were lucky that way—and deep-set dark eyes.

He looked at it, squinting. "I'm no good without my glasses."

Joe found them on the counter in the kitchenette. "Here you are, sir."

Frank put them on, blinking hard a few times before focusing in on the picture again. "Let me see…"

I held my breath as I waited. It looked like Joe was holding his, too, when I looked at him.

Frank's hand started to shake. "Oh. Oh." He shook his head. "No. I can't. No." He dropped the photo, which fluttered to the floor.

"Mr. Welburn, it's all right!" I was horrified. And even more so when he started to cry. "I didn't mean to upset you!"

"No, I won't. I won't." He dissolved into broken sobs. "No. It's not. No."

I was at a total loss and hated myself for doing this to him. "I'm so sorry. I'm so sorry! We'll go now. I'm so sorry."

The door opened, and in came the aide. Funny how she wasn't so kind and warm anymore as she pushed her way past us. "I'm going to have to ask you to leave."

"Of course. I'm so sorry. We're sorry. I didn't know—" I was still babbling incoherently as Joe pulled me from the room.

"We're sorry," he called out one last time before closing the door, leaving us alone in the hall.

"Man, that was... I didn't mean..." I wiped my eyes. "I should've known."

"There was no way you could know. Come on. Let's go. It was worth a shot." He handed me the photo as we started our trek to find an exit. "Didn't wanna leave that behind."

At least one of us was thinking clearly. I wanted to go back to bed and start the entire day over again. With far fewer mistakes this time.

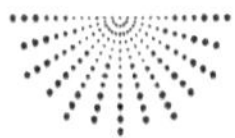

CHAPTER TWENTY-ONE

"He burst into tears?" Deke blew out a long sigh through pursed lips. "Wow. That's awful. You must've been—"

"Mortified. I was downright mortified. I felt like the world's worst person. I never imagined it would make him feel that way. Why didn't I think about it?"

"Because you're not psychic, and you can't expect yourself to be."

I cracked open a crab claw and picked out the meat with a tiny fork. "Still. I could've been gentler with him. Here I am, thinking about him as that young man who abandoned his girl. He's an old man now. He lives in a memory care unit, for God's sake. What was I expecting?"

"You didn't know he would react that way," he reminded me. "Sure, you took a chance. But it wasn't your fault."

"I have a bad habit of steamrolling my way through situations, don't I?" I cracked another claw.

"You're enthusiastic."

"You're the second person in the past couple of days who's said that. And I'm not sure I like it, to be honest."

Deke chuckled. "Why not? Do you know how rare it is, finding somebody who gets enthusiastic about things? We live in such a jaded world, full of jaded people. People who sink under the weight of their responsibilities. People who're afraid to live with passion."

"You think I live with passion?" I asked with a soft smile.

"Why do you think I had such a hard time staying away from you after we first met?" he asked. For once, he wasn't teasing or trying to be cute with wordplay. "Why do you think I went through all the trouble I went through for you? People gravitate toward you. It's a gift you have."

I fiddled with the crab claw.

He went back to his platter of crabs with a shrug. "Granted, it can be infuriating at times."

"I knew it. You were being too nice."

"But I mean it. Really, I do. There's nothing to be ashamed of, and certainly nothing to second-guess in your personality. You're great just the way you are."

"Even if I upset a poor, old man?"

"You couldn't have known. Besides, the staff are probably trained when it comes to handling residents with memory issues. I'm sure they get upset regularly."

"Oh, awesome. I'm the girl who upset the guy with memory issues."

"You didn't know he had memory issues when you first got there! Emma, give yourself a break. You can't hold yourself responsible for everything that ever happens. Your heart is always in the right place, that much I know for sure.

You're a good person. Everybody does things they regret later on. People make mistakes. Nobody expects you to be perfect."

"Why does it seem like I make more mistakes than everybody else?" I wasn't joking, either. In fact, I felt a little choked up as I stared across the table to Deke.

"Because you actually try things. You're always out there, trying your best. Other people live small. They're afraid to try. They're afraid to do something other people might call foolish. I admit, I thought you were a misguided fool back when you wanted to help Chef Robert. I thought, what good can one person do? It wasn't like you were a cop. You had no real expertise when it came to things like that. The odds were stacked against him. I was sure you would end up regretting trying to help him. But here we are. Robert's restaurant is going strong, and everybody knows he was innocent. Thanks to you. You didn't give up, no matter how bad things looked. I know there's a lesson in there some-where for people like me who tend to be jaded, thinking we've seen it all and heard it all."

"My instincts are usually on point when it comes to people and situations like that," I mused.

"Okay, Emma Harmon. What do your instincts tell you about this situation? You met the lawyer. You've seen what kind of person he is. And you said it yourself, he was sketchy. He did everything he could to avoid giving you a straight answer when it came to what happened to Milli-cent's money. What are your instincts telling you?"

"They're telling me he's lying about something. He prob-ably didn't do the work it took to find Millicent's son.

Maybe he really was upset about not getting his name included in the will. The way he talked about himself? Their so-called relationship? How close they were, how she didn't have any friends besides him? I can only imagine how he must have wormed his way into her life, hoping to earn her trust and respect and affection."

"It wouldn't be the first time a person glommed onto a wealthy, elderly man or woman."

"Which means if her son is out there somewhere, odds are he has no idea he has all this money waiting for him."

"If that son is still alive."

"Of course. I want to believe he is."

"So do I," he grinned. "It would be nice to see somebody's life change that way. It's like something out of a book or a movie. A guy works hard his whole life, and then finds out he was the heir to a fortune for so many years."

I couldn't help it. When he put it that way, my hands tingled. "I want to make that happen for somebody," I admitted. "Not for myself. This has nothing to do with me. I want to help change somebody's life for the better."

"Now, granted. I hate to be the rain cloud, but money doesn't always change people's lives for the better. It just gives them more money."

"You're right. I shouldn't expect miracles or anything like that. But it would be nice, wouldn't it?" Then, I laughed. "I'm sure twenty million is a drop in the bucket to you."

"I wouldn't take it that far," he said, cracking a crab leg like an expert.

Unlike me, he didn't send little bits of shell flying in all directions. I'd been eating crabs this way my entire life, but I had never managed to find a way to not make a mess of myself and the surrounding area and maybe even people sitting nearby.

"So. What do you think of this place?" I reminded myself that my entire life couldn't revolve around other people's problems. Here I was, with Deke, and we were supposed to be having an actual date this time. "Not as fancy as the place we went to before, but the food is good."

He took a look around the open restaurant, operating off what used to be an abandoned pier which sat out over the ocean. It wasn't the least bit fancy. There wasn't a table-cloth in sight. We both wore bibs to protect our clothes, so the romance factor was slim to none.

"Honestly? This is much more my speed. Sitting here, with the breeze ruffling my hair, eating some of the freshest seafood I've ever tasted. Oh, and the company's not that bad, either."

"Even if I keep hitting you with bits of shell?" I winced.

"It's part of the ambiance," he laughed. "Really, I love it. This was a great suggestion."

"I'm glad." It seemed like we did better together when we weren't trying to be something, when neither of us was trying to put on any sort of pretense. All there was to do was laugh and enjoy each other's company.

"So, what's on the horizon for you? Any assignments coming up from Marsha?"

I wiped my fingers with a wet napkin, nodding. "She wants to send me to Austin next, and I'm looking forward to it. After that, I think I'm going to the Vineyard." I lifted my shoulders up near my ears, pursed my lips and batted my eyes. "Like I'm a fancy person."

"And we both know you're not that," he joked.

"Hey." I dropped the act. "I am, so. When I feel like it and the opportunity arises."

"Anyway, that sounds nice."

I nodded, grinning eagerly. "Yeah, I get to see how the other half lives. I told her I'm more open to the idea of international assignments, and she said she would pass one my way the next time something came up."

"That's terrific! Maybe I'll see if I can get in on the Vineyard assignment."

"That would be awesome." And it would be. We worked well together, and any excuse to spend more time with him was a welcome one. Maybe that was how we were best, come to think of it. Just like tonight, in this casual setting, we meshed well without any expectations or pressures. It was better to go with the flow and enjoy ourselves and each other when we had the chance.

I wasn't sure what that meant for any sort of future relationship, but it made the present moment much more pleasant.

Once we were finished eating and cleaned ourselves up as best we could, we went for a stroll on the beach. There were still a few people playing in the waves, relaxing on the sand, but for the most part the crowds had thinned to nearly nothing. At this time of night, people were more interested in getting something to eat and strolling along the boardwalk, which many of them were doing right that very minute.

Deke bent to take off his shoes and roll up his pants. The water was pleasantly warm, swirling around our feet as we walked the shoreline hand-in-hand. It was idyllic, absolutely perfect, the gold of the late sun matching the gold in his eyes.

"You know, I've been thinking. Along the lines of what we argued about the other day. I know I already apologized," he was quick to add when my mouth opened in preparation for an argument, "but I feel it bears repeating. You don't owe me anything. I love spending time with you, that's all I know."

"I love spending time with you, too," I assured him. "Unless you're giving me a hard time about something, in which case you can walk off into the water and never come back."

He burst out laughing. "You are so harsh." He chuckled, shaking his head.

"No. I'm enthusiastic, remember?"

He stopped suddenly, pulling me close. The sea breeze teased strands of hair out of the braid I'd woven it into. He smoothed it all back, freeing my face before taking my chin in his hand. "And you're a challenge. I've always been a sucker for a challenge."

I smiled up at him. "I wouldn't want to make things too easy for you," I teased. Anything else I would've followed that up with was cut short by Deke's kiss. Talk about your idyllic moments.

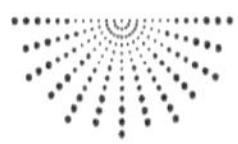

CHAPTER TWENTY-TWO

"So, Raina's on her way down to Maryland to see Nate."

"I'm so glad things are working out between them," Mom gushed. "Raina is such a nice girl."

"She's the best. And he's a really good guy. How often do you think it works out that a person ends up with their childhood crush?" I mused as I pulled a cinnamon scone from the bakery case and handed it over to a customer.

"More often than you might think," she chuckled. That was when I remembered. Dad had been the older boy in the neighborhood, living across the street from Mom and her family. That was how they'd met, as kids.

No wonder she still took their separation and divorce so hard. He'd been part of her world for literally almost her entire life.

At least she managed to seem upbeat about it, like the reminder didn't hurt her too badly. Was she starting to heal, finally? There was no telling how long it would take a person to heal from something like that. I definitely didn't begrudge her the time she took.

It would be so good to see her get back into her life, her full life. She was hardly an old woman. There was plenty of juice left. I'd noticed Nell walking down Main Street with Rance twice since we'd first met up after dinner with Deke. She wasn't letting age hold her back. And Trixie dated regularly; men of all ages, in fact. She didn't discriminate.

I tried to imagine Mom in her place and that was a bad idea, so I redirected the topic. "Anyway, it was good to spend time with Raina. It's not easy, maintaining adult friendships. Is it?"

"Especially with the sort of friends you have, always running around all the time. I guess I have it easier with Trixie and Nell being here with me, settled down. Even so, I still have to remind myself to make time for them. You're right, it isn't easy." Mom thanked the latest customer before smiling widely for the next in line.

But he didn't smile back. In fact, he was scowling. "I'm here to talk to Emma Harmon." He had a rough sort of voice, like the sort of man who was used to shouting at people. That didn't exactly endear him to me.

I exchanged a worried look with Mom. "I'm Emma Harmon," I murmured with my heart in my throat. What in the world could this be about?

If he didn't look like somebody who was out for blood, he would've been an attractive, older man. He had a nice, deep tan, which set off his silvery hair. His eyes were a pale blue, like they'd been bleached by the sun that had darkened his skin. He looked healthy, vigorous.

Vigorously furious as he turned to me. "Just what business did you have with my uncle yesterday? What did you think you were doing, barging into his room like that?"

"What's this about, Emma?" Mom asked, taking my side in a protective stance. "And I would have you know, sir, that no matter what the situation is, you have no right to barge into my place of business and air your grievances in such a manner. If you can't be polite, I would ask you to leave."

How she managed to deliver that little speech in such a deceptively calm tone of voice was a mystery to me. Then again, she wasn't the one he was angry with.

And she definitely wasn't the one still carrying guilt after the debacle that was the visit to Frank Welburn's room.

The worst of the morning rush had passed, so I turned to Mom with an apologetic smile though I knew she could handle a crowd. "I'll step outside with him," I whispered.

"What is this all about?" she hissed, shooting the man a dirty look. She'd gone full Mama Bear.

"I'll explain later, I promise." I then followed this perfect stranger out to the sidewalk. At least he would be less likely to do anything dangerous while we were out in public. Or so I hoped.

"Okay, first let me apologize." I sat on a bench near the curb, under the shade of a leafy tree. We were still in plain view of everyone inside the café. I knew that would make Mom feel better, if she could keep an eye on me. "I never meant to upset—"

"I don't care what you meant to do. What you did took the staff an entire day to calm him down. You had no right to be there. You don't even know him." He wouldn't sit, choosing instead to stand like the difference in our heights would intimidate me. If that was what he intended, he managed it pretty well, since I couldn't shake the feeling of getting yelled at as a little girl by my dad.

I pressed my palms together, tucking them between my knees. They were slick with sweat. What did I think would happen? Did I imagine I would be able to get away without explaining myself to somebody? That aide at the retirement home had mentioned a nephew. I should've known she would've called him. And just my luck, she remembered the name I gave her when Joe and I first entered the lobby.

"Can I ask your name, please? It's just that I like to know who I'm talking to."

"Charlie." His voice was gruff, his brow furrowed like he didn't really want to tell me his name but felt like he didn't have a choice.

"Thank you, Charlie." It took an effort to make my voice stop shaking. I was never very good when it came to this sort of thing. Being yelled at, being the villain even when I had decent intentions. "I am so sorry that I upset your uncle yesterday. Really, that was the last thing I wanted to do."

"What did you do? He couldn't even tell anybody what it was that got him so upset. What did you do to him?" His voice rose in volume with every word until he was practically screaming in my face. I shrank back out of pure reflex, wondering if it was such a good idea to talk to this man at all.

A glance inside the café showed Mom watching, furious. She held up the receiver to the café's land line, eyebrows raised. Did I want her to call the cops? I shook my head.

The cops came, anyway. Rather, one cop.

"Hey! What are you doing?"

I had never been so glad to see Joe in my entire life. Which was saying something, since he tended to show up just when I needed him.

"What's it to you?" Charlie demanded, whirling on him. "Why don't you mind your own business?" He spoke and carried himself like a man who was uses to taking care of business. He dressed well enough, but there was something course about him. The sort of guy who made his living working outdoors, joking and laughing with the guys, cracking open a beer at the end of the day.

"This is a friend of mine, and while my jurisdiction is up in Paradise City, I am a police detective." Joe stared him down, his jade green eyes narrowing dangerously. *Your move*, he seemed to say without speaking a word.

Charlie backed down, but just a little. "I just want to know why she was there yesterday. That's all. My uncle cried the entire rest of the day, it took hours to calm down. I finally had to go and do it myself. And even then, it took me ages. I've never seen him like that, never in my life." He was shaking, enraged.

And scared.

That was what cleared everything up for me, when I realized how scared he was for his uncle. He cared about the poor old guy.

"Sir, I didn't mean him any harm. All I did was show him a picture of him and a girl from a long time ago. That's it. I wanted to know if he remembered her. Granted, I didn't know when we arrived that his memory is failing. I'm so sorry I intruded on him, really."

"We both did," Joe piped up. "I know this girl. She never meant any harm."

The man's shoulders sank. He rubbed his face with one hand. "I'm sorry. I'm not a bad guy, and I don't go around yelling at girls. If my wife was still alive, she would've stopped me from driving down here. I saw red. There's lots of people who'd like to take advantage of an old man who can barely remember what day it is."

He sat on the other end of the bench, leaning forward with his head in his hands. "You don't know the stress I'm under sometimes."

"I can't imagine. I'm sorry I added to it."

"I'm sure you didn't mean to." He turned his head slightly. "Why'd it matter if he remembered the girl in that picture? What, was she your grandmom or something?"

"I wish," I snorted. "No, she was Millicent Montbatten, who used to live here."

"Montbatten." He frowned, straightening. "Yeah, I've heard that name. I think my granddad worked for them."

"As a gardener, I heard."

"Right, right. Third generation, right here." He held up a hand, smirking. "Though I prefer landscaper." No wonder he had that killer tan.

"I've been researching Millicent's life," I explained with a look to Joe. "I found that photo of her, along with another one, tucked into books that must've belonged to her but ended up donated to my sister's shop after Millicent died. It's really as simple as that. The two of them were on the beach together one day. They both looked happy and young and carefree."

He smiled for the first time since I'd met him. "It's funny. I have a hard time imagining him like that. He's had a hard go of it. Thanks to me, mostly."

"Why you?" I asked, careful to be gentle. I didn't want to come off like I was prying, but anything I could learn about this mysterious man would be helpful.

Just what sort of person was he? There had to be more to him than just a cad who'd used and discarded a girl once she got pregnant.

"I was a handful. My parents died when I was a toddler. I barely remember them, no matter how hard I try. Of course, the passage of time doesn't help things. He raised me, rather than letting me go to an orphanage. He always said it was the least he could do."

To think of it. He'd run away from his responsibility to Millicent, but then ended up caring for his nephew. Like karma wouldn't allow him to run away for long.

"That's a shame, I'm sorry about your parents."

"I made out pretty okay, believe me. He was a good uncle. Still is. Strict, you know? Hard on me. Old school, like the kids say today. I rebelled, like we were all doing in those days. Grew my hair out, the whole thing. Got in a little trouble here and there. He always took me back every time I ran off. I figure the least I can do for him now is make sure nobody hurts him or takes advantage of him when he's not all there anymore."

"It's that bad?" Joe asked. He'd calmed considerably and was finally starting to sound more like a human.

"He has good days, don't get me wrong. But yeah, it's getting worse. I go in to see him a few times a week to make sure he's okay. Not that I don't trust the staff, but you never know. When my wife was sick—just in the hospital, mind you, not in a home like that—her things would sometimes mysteriously walk off while she was sleeping."

"I'm sure that can be a real problem," I mused. This was a good man, and to my surprise Frank sounded like a good man, too. Like he'd done everything he could to make up for his big mistake by taking care of a rebellious nephew.

"Anyway, when Bridget called yesterday to say he was in a state and you were the one who made him that way, I looked you up and came down as soon as I could this morning. I was really fixing to give you a piece of my mind."

"And you did." I grinned. "But it's okay. I would've done the same thing."

He jerked his chin toward the café. "That's your mother in there?"

"Yes. It's her place."

"She's tough," he chuckled. "I'm glad you brought me out here. I thought she might take a rolling pin to my head or something. Like I said, my wife would've talked me outta doing this if she was alive. Women usually have more sense about these things."

"Sometimes. I never should've visited your uncle yesterday. I really am sorry for upsetting him."

"It happens. He gets upset over plenty of things I can't understand." He stood, shaking Joe's hand. "My apologies."

"No need," Joe assured him.

"I'll drive back out to see him now, make sure he's okay,"

Charlie said. "Thanks for not holding an old man's temper against him."

"I don't. No worries." Since he was in such a good mood now, I figured it was worth a shot. "Would you mind taking my number? Just in case he does remember something. I know I'm being a pain—"

"You're not. Like I said, he has his good days, too." He pulled out a flip phone; it was precious, it really was, just like the little clip attached to his belt to hold it. And entered my number. "And tell your mother I'm sorry. I'd go in and tell her myself, but like I said. Rolling pin." He chuckled as he replaced his phone in its clip.

I was laughing as we shook hands, and stood next to Joe as Charlie walked away. "I can't imagine how stressful it must be, taking care of somebody in that condition," I whispered. "Always worried somebody's taking advantage of Frank. And he's a widower, too. Poor guy."

"At least we know Frank seems like a decent person," Joe offered.

"Which doesn't add up, does it?" I turned to him, frowning. "That's not the guy who'd abandon his girlfriend. You saw how he looked at her in that picture. Like she hung the moon."

"A baby can change a lot of things."

I couldn't help but think of Holly and my father. "Yeah. No kidding."

CHAPTER TWENTY-THREE

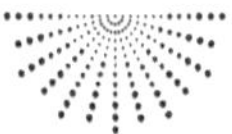

"You really don't have to hang around." Darcy finished shelving an armful of new books before turning to me. "I'm sure Lola would like to go home and rest there."

"Not after you spent the night last night, helping me with her. The least I can do is help you stock before closing." Lola was snoozing away in her bed behind the counter, anyway, so it wasn't like she cared. She was taking well to the cast, though watching her walk with that leg held carefully in the air broke my heart every time.

It would be a long month for both of us.

Foot traffic on Main Street was starting to quiet down. Right on schedule, too, with it being nearly eight o'clock. There was way too much fun to be had on the boardwalk.

"It's a shame what happened with Frank," Darcy sighed, leaning against one of the bookshelves. "I mean, all the way around. Even if he did abandon his girlfriend and baby, nobody deserves that sort of ending."

"I know. At least he has somebody who cares enough to

check in with him. Not everybody has that." I pulled another stack out of a box and started to shelve the books. "I hope I do when the time comes. At this rate, I won't. Who'd wanna put up with me for that long?"

"Oh, knock it off." She snickered. "I bet Joe would. He's that sort of guy. Stand-up. Solid."

"Stop putting ideas in my head. Are you collaborating with Mom on this? Did she tell you what to say?"

She threw her hands into the air. "No! Dork. I'm capable of my own observations and opinions, and I see what I see. That's all."

"If you say so," I muttered, totally not believing her. "No, he'll go back to work next week or later this week or whenever he's supposed to, and he'll forget all about me in favor of his job. Which I guess is the way it should be. Same with Deke. I'm fun when a guy has time on his hands, but after that?"

I didn't get the chance to finish my thought, nor did my sister have the chance to argue with me. The door opened and a new customer stepped into the shop. "I hope I'm not here too late."

Darcy's jaw just about hit the floor. It was a good thing she wasn't holding any books, because she would've dropped them on her feet.

Holly didn't venture any further into the store, only far enough that the door would close behind her. She folded her hands, chewed her lip, and looked monumentally uncomfortable. But she'd made the attempt. That much, I had to give her credit for.

Instead of saying a word to her, Darcy turned to me. Her jaw snapped shut. Her eyes narrowed.

"What?" I asked. "You have a customer."

"I was hoping you might carry baby books someplace around here," Holly offered. Boy, was she nervous, right down to the tremor in her voice. I caught her eye and tried to encourage her without saying anything.

Darcy stammered. "Uh. Um. Yeah, we do. I can show you where we stock them."

"That would be nice. Thanks."

When my sister wasn't looking, I gave Holly a thumbs up. So far, so good.

I then walked around the counter and positioned myself behind it so I could watch from afar as they made extremely awkward, extremely painful and stilted conversation. But Darcy hadn't thrown her out of the store, which seemed like a good sign.

"This one's pretty much the baby bible," Darcy said, holding up a copy of *What To Expect When You're Expecting*. "I carry it because the women who see other women picking up a copy swear by it every time, without fail. But there are a few other books here which cover different topics. And a book of baby names, too."

"Thanks. I need all the help I can get. I'm completely clueless about this. I guess I spent too much time worrying about my career and didn't bother paying attention to my pregnant girlfriends," Holly admitted.

"But here you are now, right? It happened when it was supposed to."

Even I was surprised to hear Darcy say that. I thought Holly might fall over.

Darcy's face scrunched up a little like she was fighting off a strong wave of emotion. "I'm sorry. I don't mean to get all weepy."

"No, no, it's okay. I hope—"

"It's not your fault," Darcy assured her, shaking her head while trying to keep herself under control. She was losing the battle, though, whenever her face got splotchy and her nose went red, she was good and worked up. "I told myself to treat you like any ordinary customer, but you're not. And the baby isn't some stranger."

"I really hope that's true," Holly murmured. "Because I don't want the baby to be a stranger. I don't want you to be a stranger to us, any of us. I've missed getting to know you. I don't ask you to be my best friend. I don't expect that. But I'd like us to get to know each other. And I know your dad wants you to be part of the baby's life."

Lola licked my foot when she noticed I was crying my eyes out. I wasn't sure how this would turn out when I'd first set it up. I thought Darcy might kick both Holly and me out of the store and out of her life. But I could never in a million years have imagined this.

I left them to their conversation in favor of bending to give Lola a kiss. "See? Sometimes I get things right. I needed a win. We both did, right?" She licked my hand in agreement.

Darcy joined me at the counter. "I still don't know whether or not I wanna kill you," she whispered.

"You don't. You know you don't." I grinned at Holly and

started ringing up her books. "Have you started thinking about names yet?"

"I'm afraid we'll run through at least a hundred names by the time the baby comes," she admitted. "I've always imagined naming my daughter, if I had one, after my mother. He doesn't agree."

"What's her name?" I asked.

She grimaced. "Ursula."

Darcy and I waited a split second before the laughter burst out of both of us.

Holly was a good sport about it. "Hey! It's a nice name!" she insisted, giggling.

"Yeah, but I can't help thinking about *The Little Mermaid* when I hear that name," Darcy shrugged. "I'm sorry. I shouldn't have laughed."

"Anyway, your dad hates the idea. It's gonna be a while before we reach common ground." Holly craned her neck to see behind the counter. "Oh, my gosh! He told me about the cast and everything but I never imagined! Poor sweetheart!"

"Don't let her fool you." I smirked. "She knows how pitiful she is, and she plays it for all she's worth. But I wouldn't deny her anything, especially not now."

Her face darkened. "I just about died when that awful guy came into the diner, raving about some girl and her dog. The minute he said Maltese, we knew who he meant. I hope you hit him, the jerk."

"I should've, especially since he shoved me," I grumbled, thrusting the books into a tote bag. Just thinking about it got my adrenaline pumping all over again, like I was right back in that situation. "Screaming at me that it was none of my business whether he settled Millicent's estate or not. I mean, granted, maybe it's not technically my business, but he could've come up with a straight answer. He refused."

"I heard through the grapevine that he put up a stink when the house was donated with the purpose of having it turned into a museum," Holly confided, looking from me to Darcy. "I don't know why he cared, but he did. He went to the historical society and everything."

"What's with this guy?" Darcy asked.

"Entitled," I decided. "Still thinks his opinion matters. Mad that Millicent didn't leave him anything, though to hear him talk about it he was her best friend and closest confidant. She gave him permission to call her Millie, don't you know." I rolled my eyes.

"Anyway, he's a creep. He'd better hope I don't see him around town." Holly's eyes narrowed menacingly.

"Same here," Darcy agreed. Even though we were talking about a pretty unpleasant person, it was so good to see them agreeing about something. This was the common ground they could build something on, I just knew it.

Their mutual dislike of Bernard Lewis, and the baby. What a strange world it was.

I gave Holly another thumbs up before she left. She smiled from ear to ear. I could practically feel the relief pouring off her.

"I won't pretend I'm thrilled about that," Darcy murmured when we were alone.

"I don't expect you to be thrilled. But she's nice, right? You two seemed to hit it off."

"It's easier to be nice to somebody than it is to be a jerk

to them," she sighed. "And yeah, she seems like a good person. I can tell she's sincerely excited about the baby."

"And the name Ursula," I reminded her with a chuckle.

"Yeah, let's make sure that doesn't happen. No offense to the Ursulas of the world, but that's a very big name for a very little baby." Darcy started turning out the lights while I opened Lola's stroller.

"She won't always be little—if it's even a girl," I pointed out. "It could be a boy, and this will all be moot."

"The son Dad always wanted." A sad little smile played over Darcy's lips. "I do miss him."

"I know you do. You don't have to, though."

"I know. But how do you walk back years of refusing to talk to somebody?"

The fact that she was willing to even suggest repairing their relationship made my pulse quicken. If I was dreaming, I hoped nobody woke me up.

"You just do it," I shrugged. "You just show up and do it. I know he'd be happy to see you and talk to you. No pressure, but think about it."

"I will. I mean, I do. All the time, to be honest. I'm too stubborn."

"That's something I think we all have in common." I settled Lola in just before my phone rang.

"Hmm. Joe, maybe? Or Deke? Or some boyfriend nobody knows about yet?"

"I couldn't tell you. I don't know the number." I answered anyway, though I rarely did when I didn't know who was calling.

Maybe it was instinct telling me this was important.

"Is this Emma? It's Charlie Welburn."

Like my heart wasn't already racing a mile a minute. "Charlie? Hi, yeah, this is Emma." I held up a hand to silence my sister. "What's up?"

There was a nervous edge to his voice. "Can you come? I know it's getting late, but something happened I think you'll wanna hear about."

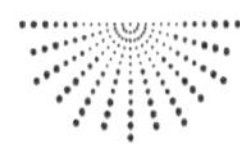

CHAPTER TWENTY-FOUR

"You can't bring a dog in here!" The girl behind the front desk at the nursing home just about jumped over the counter when she saw me wheel the stroller into the lobby.

There was no time for this. I might've been a little more strident than I need to be when I answered. "She's strapped in, she's hypoallergenic, and she has a broken leg. I can't leave her home alone. Charlie Welburn called to tell me his uncle wants to speak to me. He's having one of his clear nights when he remembers things. I have to see him."

"I don't know." She folded her arms, looking at me and my sister in turn.

"Please. We came all the way from Cape Hope and probably broke a hundred laws trying to get here before it was too late and he was too tired," Darcy pleaded. "Who knows when he'll want to talk to her again? Or if he will?"

"Charlie said it sounded important, and Frank was starting to get agitated at the idea of my not coming." I was practically jumping up and down, desperate to get to his room before the fog settled in and he couldn't remember why he wanted to see me in the first place. "Please, please, let us go."

"All right." The girl sighed. "I give up." She called out to somebody working in the office behind the front desk before stepping out to lead the way through the maze.

My palms were sweat-slicked. What did Frank want with me? What had he remembered? What was so important that we almost broke our necks getting there?

Charlie was waiting for us by the door when we arrived at the room. He looked bemused at the sight of the stroller —and my sister—but ushered us inside without protest. "He's been practically climbing the walls, waiting for you," he murmured as I passed him on my way in.

Sure enough, Frank was sitting at the edge of his bed in a pair of striped pajamas, tapping his feet on the floor. When he saw me, a look of utter relief washed over him. "Thank God you finally got here. I've been wanting to talk to you, young lady."

He sounded stern enough to stop me in my tracks. "Oh. Okay. What about?" I half expected him to ask what I thought I was doing, staying out past curfew.

Instead, he sighed deeply. "Where did you find that picture? The one you showed me?"

"You remember that?" I fished it out of my purse and held it out. "You can see it again. It was in a book, donated to my sister's store. This is my sister, Darcy."

He nodded but was more interested in the picture. There was a lamp at his bedside, and he moved closer to it so he could see better. "There she is," he whispered, his thumb stroking Millicent's image. "There she is."

That simple gesture alone brought tears to my eyes.

"So that's you in the photo with her," I murmured, moving closer. "You were her…"

"We didn't call it anything," he was quick to explain in a choked voice. I gave him a second to clear his throat. When he continued, he never took his eyes from the picture. "We didn't have to. Besides, I couldn't sport her around town in the open. The old man never would've allowed that."

"Her father?"

"George." He spat the name out like it was poison. "That pompous old thing. Never liked the notion of her running around with a boy whose father did the gardening. She had to marry a DuPont or somebody of that ilk. I was never good enough. But she got her way, let me tell you. Nobody stood in Millie's way when she wanted something."

"You were involved with that girl?" Charlie asked, amazed. "You never talked about her, Uncle Frank."

"It was too painful. Too, too painful. I wanted to, so many times." Frank gazed up at him. "You'll never know how many times."

"What finally happened, Mr. Welburn?" I asked, kneeling in front of him.

His eyes met mine, magnified slightly by his glasses. He searched my face. "You know?"

"I know," I whispered, nodding.

"Know what?" Charlie asked. "I'm confused. What are you talking about?"

"Millie's baby," Frank sighed. "Our baby."

"Your baby?" Poor Charlie sank into the armchair. "Since when did you have a baby? What's happening here? Why am I only now just hearing about this?"

"Simmer down," Frank barked, and for a second I would've mistaken him for a much younger man. I could only imagine the sort of guardian he was in his early days, when his nephew acted up. "Let me tell the story before I get confused. Millie never told me about the baby. It was her father who did it. He came to our house and fired my father on the spot. I thought it would kill him. He loved that job."

"I'm so sorry," I murmured, patting his knee.

"He died not six months later. I know it broke his heart. He'd been working there since George's father was the man in charge, practically since he was a boy. But that's not what I'm trying to tell you about. He turned on me then, screamed at me, called me every name you can imagine and some you likely couldn't. I was sure that in the end, he'd tell me I had no choice but to marry Millie."

A tear rolled down his cheek, glistening in the lamplight. "I would have. I wanted to all along, since the day I first set eyes on her. She was all I ever wanted. All I would ever want in my entire life. Nobody ever held a candle to her."

"I don't understand. If you loved her and wanted her, why—"

"Come on." His voice got that hard edge to it again. "Think. You're a smart girl if you found me after all these years. Why didn't I marry Millicent?"

It felt like an elephant settled on my chest. I slumped on my knees, settling back on my calves. Why hadn't I seen it before? "Because he wasn't there to demand you marry her. He was there to forbid it."

A grim smile. "There you are. I knew you were smart. Yes, that's why he came. He fired my father and threw a contract in my face. I was never, under any circumstances, to see or speak to or contact his daughter ever again. Told me she was engaged to a boy from Philadelphia, that once the baby was born and shipped off someplace, she'd be free to marry the sort of man she was meant to. Somebody with a future. Not some gardener's son with dirt under his nails. He'd pay me off, asked me to name my price. But he'd take it all away if I ever broke our agreement."

"I doubt you signed it without a fight."

He laughed. "Oh, I fought. I had love on my side. I was naïve, barely twenty years old. I thought I had it all figured out. Millie loved me, and I loved her, and I'd break my neck if it meant providing a good life. The life she deserved. He set me straight. The fact is, I understand him a lot better now. She would've come to resent me before long, no matter how much we loved each other right then. It wouldn't have been enough."

"I don't mean to rub salt in the wound, but she resented you anyway. I'm sorry," I winced when he gave me a sharp look. "George told her you didn't want her. She never married a boy from Philadelphia."

"I figured that out before long," he admitted.

"So why didn't you just tell her what happened? If you knew she never got married—"

"Come on, girl. Think." He leaned down, staring into my eyes. It was unnerving, but I couldn't look away. Those eyes had seen so much in almost ninety years. "What would've kept me from going to her and breaking that contract? What were the terms? What would've been important enough to keep my mouth shut?"

I couldn't think straight. My mind raced in so many directions. I struggled to bring my thoughts into focus. "Something important. Something you didn't want to lose. Money?"

He scoffed. "I'm insulted. I was insulted when he offered it to me, too."

"What then?" I grunted out of frustration.

Darcy didn't grunt, standing at the foot of the bed. She gasped. I looked up and found her clamping her hands over her mouth. "What?" I demanded.

"The baby." It was Charlie who said it. "He gave you the baby so long as you promised to keep everything quiet. And if you went to her, or he found out you tried to reach out, he'd take it away."

"Charlie…" Frank murmured. "Charlie, I—"

"You told me my parents died," he whispered, while I just about fell flat on the floor. It was Charlie all along. He wasn't Frank's nephew. He was his son, his and Millie's, all that time.

"My brother did die, along with his wife, when you were just shy of two years old. It was almost the perfect story. You remembered them, you used to spend a lot of time with your aunt during the day while I worked. I didn't have anybody else to care for you and couldn't afford anything better. When you got a little older, I told you they were your parents. You believed me."

I couldn't breathe. It was all too sad, too tragic, too much of a waste. All that time wasted. All those years.

"I hope you can forgive me," Frank whispered, his voice raspy. "My boy. I'm sorry. I was afraid he'd take you away. And by the time he died, I felt like such a fool. So many years had passed, it seemed impossible to admit the truth. I'd have to explain everything, why I'd lied so many times. All those times I wanted to tell people you were my son, because I was so proud of my boy. I still had you, even if I couldn't have her. It was the last thing I could do for Millie. Raising you."

Darcy had to sit on the bed, she was crying so hard.

Frank handed her a box of tissues. "Here you are." He smiled. "I'm sorry to make you cry."

Meanwhile, Charlie didn't know which end was up. He kept looking around the room like he was expecting a camera crew to jump out and tell him he was being pranked. "I can't believe it. I mean, I can, sorta. I always felt like there had to be more to it than you being my uncle. The way you kept taking me back, forgiving me, encouraging me. Being hard on me. You never gave up."

"I never would." Frank's voice bore a quiet dignity. "You're my son."

He looked down at me then. "It feels good to tell the truth. Thank you for giving me a reason to. I might never have found the courage, but when I saw that photo." He looked at it again, cradling it the way I imagined he might've cradled Charlie when he was just a newborn.

"I have another one. This is the one that got me started."

I pulled out the pregnancy photo and gave it to him. "They're yours. They should always have been yours."

"My goodness," he beamed. "There she is. More beautiful than ever. My beauty."

I took a deep breath and let it out slowly before speaking. This had to be done carefully, or I might end up killing both men from the shock of it.

"Charlie? Is your birthdate August twentieth, nineteen forty-nine?"

He jumped, startled. "Yeah. How did you know that?"

I leaned over and took his hand. "It's a good thing you're sitting down."

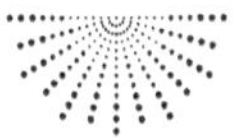

CHAPTER TWENTY-FIVE

"Thanks for sneaking us in," I whispered to Holly as stood together on the deep front porch which wrapped around the entire first floor of the Montbatten house.

"It's fine. Besides, I just stopped crying over the whole thing this morning. I'm pretty sure I cried all night long when you called to tell me what happened. I couldn't pass up the chance to let him have a look at the place." She gave me a hug. "Look what you did for him. And for Frank."

"Believe me, I didn't mean to. It just sort of... happened." We both watched as Charlie wandered the manicured lawn, examining the house his mother had lived and died in without him ever knowing.

"How's he taking it, do you think?" Holly whispered.

"I don't know. He's dazed. How would you feel if you found out everything you thought about yourself was a lie? And you were a millionaire all along and just never knew it?"

"Before or after I stopped doing cartwheels?" she dead-panned, looking me straight in the eye.

I covered my mouth to hold back a laugh. It didn't seem right, laughing at a time like this. Charlie was so solemn, taking it all in.

"I heard that Bernard Lewis character is in deep, deep trouble over this," Holly smirked. "Good. He deserves it. All these years he's been sitting on that money. He couldn't touch it, but he wouldn't let anybody else. The jerk."

"He'll never practice again," I mused. "Good riddance. I bet Millicent would've regretted letting him call her Millie if she knew the sort of guy he was."

We strolled into the house, which was just as breath-taking inside as it was from the sidewalk. Which was as close as I'd ever gotten before then. I whistled softly at the details. Exquisite plasterwork, pocket doors, stained glass windows. "At least they didn't change everything," I murmured. It was like walking around in a church. I felt that solemn.

"True. They weren't complete idiots. But they painted the floors. Can you imagine? It took a ton of effort to restore them." She shook her head in disgust. "Paint. Ugh."

"Monsters." I gave her another hug. "Would you mind if I took a minute of my own? Just to, you know…"

"Please, go ahead. I'll catch up with Charlie and tell him some of the things I've learned about this place." She went outside, and the sound of her calling out to him echoed and got smaller the further away she walked.

It was just me in that big, gorgeous house. Me and a ghost.

"Millicent?" I whispered, feeling like a total idiot even though it seemed like the right thing to do. My voice echoed off the hard floors, walls, the fifteen-foot ceiling. "I hope you can rest easy now. Your son got what you wanted him to have—or he will once things are settled. And Frank got to admit the truth. I don't know if I would've had the courage to do what he did, especially when he must've known how you'd hate him for abandoning you. He still loves you."

I wandered into the library, the shelves empty. There were boxes stacked everywhere. Probably random, attractive books that would give a nice, homey look to the room. Millie's books used to sit there. Including the books that held the keys to her heart.

I ran my hand over one of the shelves. "I'm so glad I found you," I whispered to the room at large.

~

"There they are!" Mom raised her hands, clapping, when I entered the café with Charlie in tow.

"What's this?" he asked, laughing at the sight of a cake sitting on one of the tables. Mom had written the word *Congratulations* on it in frosting.

"She wanted to do a little something for you," I explained in a soft voice. "She means well."

"This is... much more than I ever would've expected. I wouldn't expect anybody to care." He looked genuinely touched, maybe a little overwhelmed. Who could blame him?

"You always have friends here," Mom assured him. "And it isn't every day justice is served."

"Thank you," he croaked, looking around the café. Darcy was there, and Joe. Trixie, Nell, and even Rance. Lola hobbled around on three legs. I was quick to scoop her up.

Mrs. Merriweather elbowed her way to where Charlie stood. "Your mother was one of my dearest friends," she beamed, taking his hands. "She would've been proud of the fine man you've become."

I left them to talk, since Charlie wanted to hear all about his mother.

Joe was grinning, watching them as I approached. "I gotta hand it to you, Harmon. You do good work."

"Maybe there's an open spot for me on the Paradise City police force?" I suggested.

"I wouldn't go that far. I shudder to think of you with a gun."

"Shush. Anyway, I think this is my last adventure for a little while. I have a ton of work to do, and this girl here to take care of." I kissed her head and was rewarded with a million chin licks.

"I doubt it." He smirked. "Something else will fall into your lap and you won't be able to resist. You're addicted to this sort of thing. It's in your blood."

I scoffed. "Whatever. You act like you know me."

"Deke!" Mom called out, probably a little too loudly and with way too pointed a look at Joe. "It's good to see you here!"

"Mom, relax," I whispered, handing Lola off to her.

"You don't need to carry her everywhere. She'll come to expect it."

"But I don't see you putting her down, do I?" I turned to Deke with a grin. "Hey. I'm glad you could stop in."

"Me, too. Congrats on another case solved." He waved with a smile at Joe, and I was gratified to see Joe's smile in return. So things had thawed a little, thank goodness. Not like I wanted them to be besties or anything, but I didn't want them fighting over me.

Even if it was slightly exciting to think of them doing just that, as long as I was being honest with myself.

"Do you want a piece of cake?" I asked, as Charlie started slicing it.

"No, thanks. I wanted to tell you Marsha has me off on yet another assignment." He shrugged, sheepish. "What can you do?"

"Where to this time?"

"Sicily. I know, I know, my job is so difficult." He sighed deeply.

"Yeah, you're heartbroken. And I hate you."

"Maybe she'll send you there next time something comes up," he suggested. "Anyway, thanks for taking some time with me this week. I really did need to clear my head, and being with you helped."

"Any time. I mean that. Just, you know. Call first? No more of these sudden appearances in my life. My heart can't handle it."

He bent to kiss my cheek. "That's a deal. I'd better get going, my flight's in a few hours. Talk soon?"

"You know it." I watched from the window as he strolled

down the street, looking like God's gift to denim in those jeans of his. It wasn't easy to watch him go, to know it would be difficult to pin him down for long.

"You okay?" Darcy asked, standing just behind me.

"Me? Sure, of course. We worked things out. For now, it'll have to be enough to drift in and out of each other's lives." I turned to her with a wink. "This way, he can't get tired of me."

"What about that one?" She nodded to Joe, who was busy being peppered with questions by both of our aunties.

Rance stood back, watching with a grin.

"I couldn't tell you, honestly. I don't know what's going on there."

"Just listen to your heart," she advised.

"I'm a little more worried about that heart right now." I nodded to Mom, who kept exchanging looks with Charlie as he handed her slices of cake to give out. "She's blushing, for the love of Pete. And he won't stop smiling at her."

"He's way too old for her," Darcy hissed.

"That doesn't matter. Besides, even if nothing comes of it, she's noticing a man for the first time in forever. That's saying a lot."

"Jeez."

"What?" I asked, turning to her in surprise. "Isn't that a good thing?"

"Of course! It's just, you know..." She bit her lip, glancing at Mom with her brows drawing together. "She's bad enough now, when she's only trying to plan our love lives. What happens when she has one of her own?"

"I think I'm gonna need two slices of cake," I groaned.

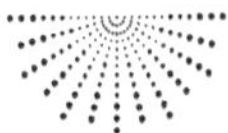

CHAPTER TWENTY-SIX

"I got a call from Charlie today," I announced while cutting up vegetables for salad. "He's already looking into another facility for his dad, closer to Cape Hope. He wants to move here. I guess he feels a connection to the town now."

"That's nice. It'll be good to have him around. He belongs here. Isn't that a strange thing to say?" Holly laughed at herself, stirring the sauce on the stove. "He's a total stranger, but it feels like this is where he should be."

"Not strange," Joe said. "His mother lived here. This is where his parents met and fell in love. Probably where they would've lived if things had been different."

"To think, they were only a half-hour from each other that whole time," I mused, shaking my head. "I could never have kept the secret for that long."

"Somehow, that doesn't surprise me." Joe snorted.

I raised my knife menacingly before bringing it down in stabby motions.

"You're in my apartment, in case you forgot," I warned, stabbing the air.

"You're bluffing. You wouldn't wanna clean my blood off the floor."

"Then I'll have to throw you out the window." I caught Holly grinning in a Cheshire Cat sort of way and pointedly ignored her.

"I have to say," she said after testing the sauce. "Yours is just as good as mine. Maybe better."

"Now I know pregnancy brain is a real thing, because there's no way that's true!"

Dad entered the kitchen, took a spoon from the drawer and dipped it into the pot. "Only one way to find out. An impartial judge."

"Impartial?" I asked, skeptical.

He blew on it. Tasted it. Closed his eyes. "Hmm. I'll leave my opinion to myself."

"Oh, come on!" I shouted.

Lola barked in agreement, standing at Dad's ankle.

"Careful," he laughed along with the rest of us. "You'll end up with sauce all over your fur." She hopped away.

I was still laughing when the bell rang.

I looked at Joe, who looked at me. We both looked at Holly, who raised her gaze to the ceiling and whispered in what sounded like Italian.

"Can you get that, Dad?" I asked, suddenly way too busy with chopping and such to be bothered to go the five feet to my front door. I said every prayer I knew in the few seconds it took for him to cross the kitchen.

"Who could it be?" he murmured, puzzled, before opening the door. And coming face-to-face with Darcy.

"Hi, Dad," she managed to choke out.

"Darcy," he breathed. "Oh, sweetie." I couldn't see his face, but I could guess what he looked like. Awestruck? Relieved?

"I thought I'd come for dinner, since Emma was having you over. I thought… here." She thrust a gift bag his way. "An early present for the baby."

He didn't take it right away. Instead, he wrapped her in a hug.

"Come on." Joe took my arm and led me to the living room window, away from the kitchen. Holly followed, wiping her eyes on her apron.

"Like my emotions aren't already off the wall," she chuckled, dabbing carefully so as not to mess up her eye makeup. "This has been a rollercoaster of a few days."

"Right? And I don't even have a baby to blame my mood swings on," I reminded her, also dabbing my eyes.

Dad had managed to pull Darcy into the apartment and close the door, but he hadn't let go of her yet. I wondered how long it would take. Maybe he'd eat dinner that way.

Not that I'd complain. And from the smile on my sister's face, I didn't think she would, either.

"You got what you wanted," Joe observed. "She made the first move."

"It's about time," I muttered, shaking my head. "Stubborn as a mule."

"It's a family trait."

"I know you're not suggesting I'm stubborn, Detective."

"No. I'm flat-out saying you are."

"You two," Holly sighed, rolling her eyes, before wiggling her eyebrows up and down at me when Joe wasn't looking.

My phone buzzed in my pocket. I was glad for the distraction, since Holly was just as determined as everybody else to make something out of Joe and me. Why couldn't we just be good friends who joked about killing each other and maybe flirted a little every once in a while? Why couldn't people leave it alone?

"Speaking of people who won't leave it alone," I muttered softly when I found a text from my mother waiting for me.

"What?" Joe asked.

"Nothing." I opened the app to read her message.

I've been thinking about that whole online dating thing. How does that work?

I closed my eyes. It had begun. Darcy would laugh herself sick when she found out, but she was still busy making up for several years of lost hugs.

It can't be that hard. Plenty of people do it. Some people even find real relationships on there. Are you seriously thinking about doing this? That's great!

She got back to me maybe three seconds later. *I'm too old for this.*

You are not! I replied. *I saw the way Charlie Welburn was eyeing you the other day. Like you were a snack.*

Emma Jane!

Good. Let her be scandalized after all the embarrassment she'd put me through over the years. This would be fun.

"What are you smiling about?" Joe asked.

"Mom wants to start online dating," I whispered. "I can't wait to torment her. I've got years of ammunition waiting to be used."

"Careful with that, though," he warned, though he was grinning. "It takes guts to get back out there. This is a huge step." I wished I didn't feel like he was talking about himself, somehow. And that he wouldn't look at me the way he did.

And that I wouldn't look right back at him the same way. Oh, boy, he had nice eyes. And nice everything else.

"Hey, there. Detective," Dad called out from across the room. "Did you tell Emma the good news?"

"What good news?" I asked. "I didn't hear any good news. What's the good news?"

"If you'd take a breath, I'd have the chance to tell you." Joe chuckled. "I worked it out just today, with your dad's help. I'm transferring to Cape Hope for the foreseeable future. To help with my stress. I rented an apartment for six months with the option to extend."

Transferred to Cape Hope. A six-month lease. To help with his stress.

His stress?

His stress?

What about my stress? Having him in town all the time, bumping into him in random places, having no excuse to stay away from him when he was right there. At least when he was in Paradise City, there were miles and miles between us. I had a reason to stay away.

Now, he'd be there in front of me.

Maybe right in front of me with other women. Did I

want that to happen? No, I most certainly did not, but I didn't have a claim on him, either.

His stress?

Another message came through. I looked down, distracted.

I need you to help me make up one of those profile thingies. I want it to be just perfect, but not too eager or desperate sounding. Can you come over later tonight to make it up with me?

"Emma? You okay?" Joe took my arm. "You don't look so good."

"Oh, I'm fine," I lied with a carefree laugh as the man I might've been half in love with smiled in relief and my wounded dog hobbled past and my dad beamed with joy at the thought of me getting together with a detective and my mom waited for a reply and I understood nothing in my life would ever run easily for more than a few minutes at a time. "Things couldn't be better."

*K*eep reading for an excerpt from the next Winnie Reed *Cape Hope Mysteries* selection.

Online dating can be murder...

Sylvia Harmon's daughters, Emma and Darcy, have finally convinced her to join the online dating scene. Except that the women in Sylvia's new beau's life seem to have been dropping like flies.

Can Emma keep out of this new mystery?

Join Emma on her next adventure with the adorable Lola, Detective McHottie. Will a certain photographer decide to make an appearance?

CHAPTER 1

There were certain situations a daughter never imagined herself living out.

Depending on the circumstances, they became more likely. A sick parent meant she might have to brace herself for the possibility of losing that parent earlier than she'd expected. A divorced parent meant she'd have to get over the idea of them finding somebody new.

I'd already been through that part. Dad and Holly were going strong, and Holly was carrying my baby brother or sister.

Still.

After all the years since my parents' divorce.

It never occurred to me that I'd be sitting in my mom's bedroom, helping her pick out an outfit for her all-important third date with a man she'd met online.

Granted, she had no idea what Darcy or I meant when we snickered about this being the third date. And there I was, thinking we were finally making a reference that wouldn't go completely over her head.

"I don't understand why you think this date is particularly important," Mom sighed, holding up one dress, then another, in front of herself. "We're just going for seafood over at Lou's."

"It's not about what you're actually doing," Darcy reminded her before rolling her eyes my way. "It's about…"

"What you're actually doing," I snickered. She swatted at me.

"I don't understand what you're talking about! Either of you." Mom shook her head. "Both of you. I thought I raised nice girls."

"You did," I insisted, winking at my sister. "And we know you know what we're talking about, or you wouldn't be accusing us of not being nice girls."

"Enough of this talk," she sniffed, turning to face us with a dress held up in front of her. "What do you think about this?"

I wanted to hide my frown, but it wasn't easy. "I think that would look nice covering your sofa." The big, flowery pattern overwhelmed her.

"It makes you look older," Darcy added, wincing when Mom threw a dirty look her way. "I'm sorry, but it's true."

"It's true," I added. "We're not trying to make you feel bad, but you're still a young woman. You should dress more youthfully."

"And your clothes are all from ages ago. When was the last time you went shopping?"

Mom dropped the dress. "Why don't I just find a shovel in the garage and dig myself a grave?"

"Mom…" I sighed.

"No, really. Since I don't deserve to live. I dress like an old lady, my clothes are outdated, and I have no hope of keeping a man interested." Mom sat on the bed with a thud. "I don't know why I'm wasting my time. I can't compete."

"Don't say that!" I threw an arm around her shoulders. "We're only trying to help. Hey, if he weren't interested, there wouldn't be any third date. He obviously likes you."

"You're the one who asked us to come and help you find something nice to wear," Darcy added. "It wouldn't hurt you to shake things up a little."

"I admit," Mom said, exhaling, "I've let things go over the years. Too busy working. I don't think about things like, you know. Updating my wardrobe." She snickered, rolling her eyes.

"You say that like it's a bad thing," I chided. "It isn't. You deserve to take care of yourself, too. Hey. I brought a few things with me, just in case."

"You can't say you let things go when you've been the same size my entire life," Darcy reminded her as I grabbed my tote bag. "I mean, you work around baked goods all day, and you never gain a pound."

"I'm on my feet all the time," Mom pointed out, eyeing the clothes I was pulling out like she expected them to attack her or something.

"You've got it going on," I said, dropping things on the flowered bedspread. She had a thing for floral prints. "You just have to. You know. Not be so afraid to show you've still got it."

"I don't know that I ever had it," she laughed. "This is so silly."

"Is not." I picked out a simple, black sheath and shooed her into the closet so she could try it on. I'd always envied the walk-in closet in the master bedroom—and it had only been half-filled since the divorce, giving her even more room.

Darcy and I exchanged a look that could only be described as exasperated while Mom changed into the dress. I looked over the pile of discarded dresses and wondered if we could donate them—or better yet, burn them.

"So this guy's pretty special, huh?" I called out as I picked through outfits I remembered from childhood.

"I'm pretty sure she wore that to your confirmation," Darcy whispered, pointing to a dress I was examining.

"Bob?" Mom called out, unaware of our giggles. "He's very sweet. A gentleman. You don't meet many of them nowadays."

"That's true, I guess. You've already met a few idiots." In the month since she'd decided to venture into the dating world again, Mom had proven to be fairly popular. And why not? She was still beautiful, a brilliant entrepreneur, and she made chocolate chip cookies to die for.

"Don't remind me. I don't want to think about any of them when I'm getting ready to see Bob."

Darcy ignored this, of course. "Gotten any calls from the

insurance guy?" He'd tried to sell Mom a life insurance policy between the appetizer and entrée courses.

"Only two. I think he finally got the message." And then there'd been the guy whose wife picked him up after dinner —they were in the process of splitting up but still living together and, evidently, still sharing a car.

I was glad this Bob person seemed like a decent guy, though I worried that her less-than-stellar experiences had made her lower her expectations to the point where anyone who didn't pose a threat or tell her she reminded him of his ex-wife or mother seemed like a catch.

The closet door opened and my jaw just about hit the floor. "Whoa. Mom. Holy cow." I held my head in my hands in case it decided to fall off.

"Mom! You're hot!" Darcy bounced on the bed hard enough to almost knock me on the floor.

Mom touched a trembling hand to her upswept blond hair, her cheeks going pink. "No, I'm not." She giggled, looking at the floor.

"But you are." I got up before Darcy knocked me on my butt and went to her. "You're always hiding your figure! Why? You look gorgeous." She had a perfect hourglass shape which my dress accentuated.

"I've seen Emma wear that dress and she's never looked that good in it."

I gave my sister a dirty look. "Thanks. Though you're right. But you didn't need to say it."

"Do I really look nice?" Mom asked, looking back and forth between us.

"You wanna know something?" I whispered. "I think you

know you do. I can tell. And I think Bob's gonna lose his mind when he sees you."

"Here." Darcy handed her a pair of red pumps. "Unless you think they're too daring for a third date."

"Shush." But she took the pumps because she wasn't stupid.

"I don't know if we can let you out of the house looking like this," I teased.

"What about poor Bob?" Darcy lobbed back with a wink. "I hope he doesn't have a bad heart. Maybe we should call him up and ask, just to be safe."

"I wanna see a doctor's report."

"Enough, you two," Mom laughed. "Go. I think I can handle putting on makeup and perfume."

"Go light on both," I advised. "You're already gonna knock him out. You want him to be able to come to eventually."

"Go, go." She shooed us out of the room, laughing softly. I couldn't get over how much younger she seemed. How much happier.

Which was why my sister surprised me by whispering, "It's a shame," as we passed our childhood bedrooms and walked downstairs.

"What is?" I whispered back.

"That she took this long to do this."

I could agree with that. "Hey, things happen when they're supposed to happen. Who knows why she was supposed to wait as long as she did? There had to be a reason. We'll find out eventually."

"Maybe this Bob guy is the one for her?" she suggested.

We puttered around the kitchen, which was where we both normally ended up. It was the heart of the house, especially since so many of Mom's recipes had been born there. Oh, the calories we'd consumed.

"I don't hate the idea, but let's not courage anything."

"Why not?" she asked, sitting on a stool at the counter. "You're the one who gave her the big idea to start dating. What's wrong with her finding the right guy?"

"I don't want her jumping into anything too soon, you know?" I sat across from her and pulled a chocolate chip cookie from the jar between us before breaking it in half.

Darcy eyed the cookie. "Well?"

"Well what?"

She held out her hand. "Are you gonna share?"

I blinked. "Um, no?"

"Normally, when a person breaks something in half, it's because they plan on sharing half with somebody else."

"That's nice." I licked both halves. "Get your own. Anyway, that's what bothers me. I don't want her jumping into anything with this Bob person just because he's the first nice guy who's come along. She's been trying to date for a month. Just one month."

"Yeah, but she's also a grown woman, not some little kid who needs to figure out the whole concept of dating and having a relationship. She knows about all that stuff." She took a cookie for herself and picked at it, thoughtful.

"That's true. I guess she knows better than anybody what she wants. Who she wants to be with."

"Besides," she added, "it's not like they're gonna get

married right away. I don't think she'd ever jump into that. Not after the divorce."

"Also true." I sighed, looking up at the ceiling like I could see through it and straight up into Mom's room. She was like a girl getting ready for a big dance—the sound of her happy humming floated our way through the thin floor. The walls and floors of the old house weren't exactly the thickest, which meant there was never any such thing as privacy when we were kids.

"What are you really upset about?" Darcy lowered her brow, looking at me in her usual no-nonsense, big sister way.

"I'm not upset."

"You are."

"Am not."

"Apprehensive, then. You're apprehensive. Why? You're usually one of the most positive people I know. You can take just about anything and turn it into a positive." She snickered. "Or bulldoze your way through it."

"I'm not a bulldozer."

"No. You drive one."

"You sound like Joe."

"Maybe Joe has a point."

"Shut up." I got up to wash my hands. "I don't even know why I ate that cookie. I'm supposed to be meeting him for ice cream later."

I pretended not to hear her snicker, but clearly I heard it because she wanted me to. "Ooh. Ice cream with the detective."

"Shut up," I said again. "It's not a date."

"I never said it was. You're the one who used that word."

"Whatever. You know what I'm trying to say. I'd appreciate you not trying to make this into something it isn't. I haven't spoken to him since I left for my trip to Austin, and he wanted to catch up."

"Mm-hmm."

I turned around and almost snapped a hand towel at her. "Enough. We're not here to talk about me. We're talking about Mom, remember?"

"Sure, sure. Whatever you say."

"Listen up." I shook the towel in her face. "I mean this. Don't act like there's anything between Joe and me. I don't need that in my life. Neither does he."

She stopped joking around, her blue eyes narrowing. "What's that mean?"

"He's been through a lot. I mean, a whole lot." I hadn't told her. I had never told anybody about Joe's past. But in the month since he'd moved from Paradise City to get his health in order and step away from the stress of his job, everybody in my life seemed more determined than ever to shove us together.

I dropped my voice to the barest whisper. "Promise you'll keep this to yourself." I then gave her a brief rundown. His wife, the accident. How he'd basically thrown himself into work since then.

Her face fell. "Oh, gosh. Poor guy. Why didn't you tell me before?"

"Because he obviously doesn't want lots of people to know. Maybe he's worried they'll feel sorry for him. I bet that's it, knowing the sort of person he is." I folded and refolded the towel just to have something to do. "I don't want people making a big deal about us being friends. He needs time. Heck, so do I. I don't want to start thinking of him that way and get all wrapped up with him when he might not be ready for anything like that. It's just as much for him as it is for me that I act stubborn and difficult about this. Okay?"

"Okay. Sure. I'll back off." There was a gleam in her eyes, though. "You do like him. Admit it."

"Of course I do. I'm not an idiot." Why bother pretending? It was easier to admit it to people I trusted, like my sister and my best friend Raina, than it was to act otherwise.

Mom's heels clicked on the wood floor as she approached. When she stepped into the kitchen, I pretended to swoon.

"Who's this supermodel?" Darcy asked.

"Stop." But our mother was glowing, absolutely radiant as she ran her hands down the length of the dress. "This really looks nice?"

"Beautiful," I confirmed, giving her two thumbs up. "And if things go well tonight and it's clear you two wanna see each other again, you have to invite Bob to visit the café so I can get a look at him."

"Yes, definitely," Darcy agreed. "I'm surprised he hasn't been in yet."

"His work keeps him busy," Mom explained. "Besides, I've wanted to avoid the gossip that you know will stir up if he comes in and people find out who he is."

I draped myself over the counter with a groan. "Wow. It's like she finally gets it."

I hope you enjoyed *Cape Hope Capers*!
For more Winnie Reed books click here!

Sign up for the newsletter to be notified of new releases.

Click on link for
Newsletter